TRANSFORMED IN WONDERLAND

WONDERLAND CHRONICLES
BOOK FOUR

DANI HOOTS

"One of the deep secrets of life is that all that is really worth the doing is what we do for others."

— Lewis Carroll

CHAPTER ONE

What were we to do now?

I held my legs close and sat near the fire, rocking back and forth. Malcolm had quickly located us a cave for the night as we figured out our next plan of action. I bit at my nail—something I didn't normally do, but I was trying everything I could to calm my nerves. None of it was working as nothing could make any of this better.

Glancing around, I wondered if this was the same cave we used when we first hid in the Dark Forest all those years ago. It was damp and dark, and I couldn't help but shiver. It wasn't too cold, but I shook from the fear I had.

The Duchess had control over Wonderland.

I heard steps coming into the cave and found that Malcolm had located some Trisings. As to where he got the jar, I had no idea. I stopped asking him questions long ago. The Dark Forest was a strange place, and I didn't eliminate the fact that he had supplies stored throughout the forest since this was where he used to live.

He set the jar down, and I watched as the fairylike creatures smacked the inside of the glass. I was sort of watching them but at the same time replaying everything that had happened. Kate… she was dead. How was that possible? How could Chase have brought her here and risked her life?

I had given the Duchess what she wanted, and yet I wasn't able to save Kate, and now all of Wonderland was under the Duchess's rule because I went against what Malcolm had said.

What the heck was I going to do?

At least Malcolm and I were able to escape, but as we ran, everything was warping and changing into what the Duchess wanted, which meant it was possible that everyone had already been brainwashed.

So all of our friends were now our enemies.

I didn't know if I could fight any of them after all of the time we had spent together. I considered them to be my best friends, so there was no way I could hurt them even if they were attacking me.

Although I did feel like slapping Chase across the face. But could I really fight him even though he had caused the death of my best friend? I had known him for a couple of years now, and we were close. He and I had so many wonderful memories. How could betray me like that?

More tears formed in my eyes. I couldn't believe what had happened. I would never forgive Chase for what he had done, yet when I thought about all that he went through and the thought of him working for the Duchess, my heart ached. Was it all a lie? Did he not actually care for me and was trying to deliver me to the Duchess? Or did he really want to run away so he didn't have to finish the Duchess's orders? And what would have happened if he had disobeyed her?

Malcolm took a seat next to me and wrapped his arm around me. "We will figure this out. We have each other. You aren't alone in this."

I leaned my head on his shoulder. "Thank you. For saving me, I mean. Even though this is all my fault. If I hadn't gone against your wishes to try to save Kate, Wonderland would still be fine. Kate might still be fine."

"It's not your fault; it's that stupid cat's."

"But I still should have listened to you. I shouldn't have just run off on my own. I just wanted to—" More tears. Would this crying ever stop? I wiped my face and took a deep breath.

Malcolm squeezed me tighter. "I understand. I'm sorry it ended the way it did. We will do what we can."

"Which is what? How will only two of us be able to go up against everyone in Wonderland? Am I wrong to believe that all of our friends are now under the complete control of the Duchess and are searching for us as we speak?"

Malcolm didn't answer as he intertwined his fingers with mine. It was clear he didn't know what we were going to do either. It was different when everyone was under the trance made by Morpheus, as there were seven of us. But now it was just us two, and we were against those who could stop us, like Davis and Melvin. We would have to figure something out.

"We will save Wonderland," Malcolm finally answered. "We always do. Even if the others have been brainwashed—or whatever you want to call it—they might be able to break free. I think as long as we kill the Duchess, it will all be fine."

I nodded even though I didn't know how I felt about using such violence. "Kill the Duchess. You make it sound so easy."

"Well, that's what this land is like—or used to be like. With the Kingdom of Hearts, I used to have to kill all the time. Luckily that ended for quite a long time."

I shook my head. "I'm sorry. I didn't mean…"

He stroked the top of my hand with his thumb. "I know you didn't, but don't worry about having to kill anyone. I will do it."

I didn't know how to respond. It was a bad situation as I didn't like the idea of killing as an answer. The Duchess was, however, supposed to be executed, so her sentence was already determined. But the idea of making Malcolm do the dirty work because of something that was my fault didn't sit well with me. I doubted I could take a life, and as he mentioned, he had killed many in the past.

But I didn't want him to have to relive his past

demons. I wished to help him move on.

Noticing I wasn't going to respond to what he said, he diverted the subject. "Do you think you will be able to sleep? I know this cave isn't that comfortable, but it's all we have until morning. Then we should be able to reach my old home."

"I am tired. I don't think I've slept in over thirty-six hours if I'm honest."

Malcolm shifted and leaned against the cave wall. "Lay your head on my lap, and you can sleep with at least some kind of pillow."

I blushed and wanted to protest as it didn't seem comfortable for him, but I really didn't want to sleep on the ground. I leaned over and rested my head on the side of his leg and closed my eyes. I quickly fell asleep as he stroked my hair gently.

When I awoke, I found Malcolm was still asleep. It was strange—he always was awake before I was. I smiled, as I liked seeing his gentle face. He seemed at peace—something I hadn't seen in quite some time. He usually was stressed and worried about whatever task he had been assigned—or at least that was what it seemed like. After a few moments, he stirred. He blinked a few times and then grinned.

"Good morning."

For an instant I had forgotten everything and was happy—I was happy the two of us were close like this, and I wished it could go on forever. I wished I could wake up like this every day. Then I remembered we were in the Dark Forest, hiding from the entire Wonderland Kingdom. My happiness faded as quickly as it had come.

"Good morning."

Malcolm stretched. "We should probably head to my house in the Dark Forest for the time being. Then we can figure out what to do next."

I raised an eyebrow. "Why didn't we stay in the home last time we were here?"

"Because we weren't going to stay in the Dark Forest. We were moving through it."

That was fair. But now we were stuck here until we figured out a plan. "Well then, it sounds like we should head out there."

He nodded. "Keep your katana near. You never know what is going to attack next."

I put my hand on the hilt. That was true. We had learned that many times before. I didn't want to have to face those beasts again, but I couldn't really complain —it was better than the alternative. Maybe. Hopefully.

We headed out, and I wished that I had some snacks on me. Malcolm was able to pick some plants and berries along the way and assured me that they weren't poisonous, but that was Uncle Iroh said before he poisoned himself. Malcolm had lived there for a long time, though, so I knew he wasn't lying, but I couldn't help but be a bit hesitant. This was the Dark Forest— one would assume that everything was poisonous. The berries were quite tart, but they were something to eat, so I didn't complain.

As we made our way through the forest, I heard the familiar roars and growls of what sounded like large creatures around us. I stayed close to Malcolm, practically stepping on his heels as we moved forward. He never made a comment as I almost pulled him down a couple of times. He didn't seem bothered by the sounds of the creatures around us. Perhaps he knew they wouldn't hurt him. Perhaps they knew to leave Malcolm alone as he used to live there.

I couldn't imagine living in the Dark Forest for what I gathered had been years if not decades before the first Alice came and destroyed the Heart Kingdom. It would seem like you'd be scared for your life every single moment of the day. Perhaps after a while, you'd just get numb to it all. That would explain why Malcolm appeared calm no matter what we faced.

As we moved farther through the forest, Malcolm collected some leaves and stuck them in a bag in his pocket. He did that a few times before I questioned what he was up to.

"What are those for?"

He smiled. "You will see."

I wasn't sure if I should be excited or afraid. He seemed at ease in the Dark Forest, and while I understood he spent a lot of time there, it still freaked me out a bit. Only months before, I had witnessed him kill Morpheus, and yet I had no fear of him. I supposed it was because I knew he wouldn't hurt me but would always keep me safe. Morpheus was a murderer, and Malcolm's old job was to execute those in the Dark Forest. Morpheus knew this, and that was why he made Malcolm chase him out there—so I would witness what he once was. But after seeing what all of Wonderland was capable of, was I really one to judge? There was still a lot I didn't know about this place.

We made it to the table with the teacups, which I had

visited a few times now. This was where Malcolm killed Morpheus—this was where it all went down.

Malcolm stopped and stared at the table for a moment. I was about to say something when he turned and smiled. "Right this way."

He pushed back some of the brush, and there stood a small home. I couldn't believe what I was seeing— there was a house right behind the table that I had never noticed before. Everything was always so overgrown I thought the mound was just a bunch of moss or a dead creature or something.

Malcolm laughed as he saw my dropped chin. "I figured you didn't notice. Yeah, it was here the whole time." He opened the door and whistled like one would to a dog. "Spider. Get out."

I heard a hissing noise, and then the giant spider scurried away. I quickly pulled my katana out and pointed it at the spider.

"That thing is back!"

Malcolm shook his head. "It won't hurt you—not if I am around. But don't go near it on your own."

"So I learned."

I wasn't going to go near it either way. I kept my katana out for good measure and followed Malcolm inside. I gasped, as I couldn't believe my eyes. It appeared unlike anything I thought it would. There were teapots and teacups, cozies hanging on the walls, and the area was lined with bookcases. It almost appeared like an old lady's home.

Maybe this wasn't out of left field, as Malcolm did like his tea, but it wasn't completely what I imagined. I didn't know what I would have expected.

It was rather clean, which made little sense. Perhaps the spider was keeping it clean. That wouldn't make sense in my world, but this was Wonderland—nothing ever made sense.

"Take a seat. I will make some tea with the leaves I picked."

So that was what he was doing. I should have known. I chuckled a little as I took a seat on the floral couch, still on the lookout for spiders. So far I hadn't seen any.

Malcolm made some tea and brought it out on a little tray. The cups were all decorated with flowers like one would see at a British tea shop. I took a sip, and it tasted herbal and rather sweet. It was delicious.

Sitting down across from me, he sighed. "So we will stay here until we figure out what to do next. Does that sound like a plan?"

I nodded. It was really all we could do at that point. At least we had a cozier place to wait.

CHAPTER TWO

It was hard to sleep in the Dark Forest even though I had an actual bed now. I felt like it was a bit worse, actually, as it was a fake sense of security. That, and I worried that the spider would come in while I was sleeping and try to eat me. I didn't want to wake up encased in webbing. It was a worry that I never knew I had until now.

Malcolm and I shared a room at least, as one of the rooms had two small beds. It was the room Melvin and Davis had used when they lived with Malcolm. I could only imagine what Davis was like with all the monsters roaming around. Maybe that was why he was described as drunk in the original story—I know if I had to stay there longer than a few days, I might turn to the bottle as well.

As I imagined what life was like for the three of them, I could hear Malcolm slightly snoring from across the room, which made me feel a little better. If he was at ease, then there was nothing to worry about. Then again, he always seemed to be at ease when scary things were going on. At least right now I could take comfort in knowing he would keep me safe.

I shifted in the bed and stared up at the ceiling. I couldn't get over the fact that this place was still clean. I imagined the spider in an apron with rubber gloves cleaning and tried not to laugh. Perhaps that wasn't what happened. Maybe the home was enchanted, as I wouldn't put it past Malcolm to do something like that. He mentioned having powers that he couldn't use without getting in trouble in Wonderland. I needed to remember to ask him about it now, as it wasn't like they weren't going to arrest him already.

The fact that he escaped with me made me happy. I didn't believe I would have been able to figure out any of this alone. I wondered what would have happened if

I had stayed—whether or not I would have died or if I would have served the Duchess or not. I had a feeling the odds were that I would have disappeared. I was too much of a liability to her. I was the only one who could bring her destruction.

Which was why I knew I had to stop this.

Worst-case scenario, I would eventually disappear. Best-case scenario, I stopped the Duchess, saved Chase, and brought back Kate, but then what? Would I return to my world, or would I have to stay here? Everything was still up in the air, and I didn't know what to expect.

But at least I had Malcolm. At least I wasn't alone.

I took slow, deep breaths and focused on listening to Malcolm snore. After a bit, I found myself drifting off to sleep.

I woke to find Malcolm sitting on the bed. I smiled as I looked up at him. He gently caressed my face.

"Good morning, beautiful."

I didn't know how to respond after everything. It was, in fact, not that great of a morning given where we were, but it made me feel good that he was there, giving me his smile. "Good morning."

"I decided it would be best to wake you before I went

and found something to eat so you didn't wake up alone. But if you wanted, you can join me."

That was a hard choice: go outside and deal with the Dark Forest, or stay here alone and worry about Malcolm's safety and whether that spider would come back. Actually, that was an easy choice. "I think I will go with you."

"I figured. Come, I will teach you about the plants in this area. They are quite spectacular."

I got up but didn't need to change as we slept in our clothes. I straightened them out and ran my hands through my hair a few times, hoping it was somewhat nice and not all over the place like short hair usually was in the morning. People always thought it was easier, but many times it wasn't.

I followed Malcolm outside and found that it still appeared dark out but only due to the foliage. Light barely peeked through now, and I could make out the different trees and the table outside the house.

Malcolm picked a few leaves. "You would be surprised how many of the plants in the forest are actually quite edible. It's the creatures that you have to be worried about. That doesn't go for all the plants, both here and in the forest throughout Wonderland, but it's still pretty easy to identify them here."

He showed me the plant and explained what to look for to identify the plant.

"It sounds easier than it is in my world. There're a lot of plants that look alike, and it's easy to pick the wrong thing. I have always been too scared to ever wild harvest."

"I agree. If you don't know what you're doing, then don't pick plants. But I've been doing this for quite some time, so I definitely know what plant to pick."

I nodded. "Of course."

"And also," he added, "I started a veggie garden a long while ago. Perhaps some stuff is still growing from that."

He picked some of the plants and berries that were growing around the house and pointed out ones that were poisonous. He was right. It was very clear which ones were poisonous from their color and leaf types. The berries that had spots were ones to skip over. Easy enough. I just wished it was that easy in my world.

We moved over to where his vegetable garden used to be, and I couldn't believe my eyes. It looked like a disaster area with random zucchini and tomatoes growing all over.

He grinned. "It's still growing! I wonder if the spider grew them to use as bait."

I peered around again for that creature but didn't see any sign of it. Malcolm picked some vegetables, and we headed back to his home, which was still in viewing distance.

"Feel free to relax while I make something to eat," Malcolm said as we walked inside.

"You're able to cook in the middle of the forest?"

He nodded. "Yes, energy works a bit different here. It is quite nice. You must have been tired yesterday and didn't notice the lamps and lights are, in fact, on right now."

I glanced around. Sure enough, they were.

"Huh."

"So make yourself at home. It won't take long."

I nodded and went over to the couch and took a seat. I still couldn't believe how many cozies and teacups he had hanging around the walls. Where did he even get those? Was he able to go into town when he lived out here? Or did he send others to pick them up? I wanted to ask but felt it would come across weird, so I decided to just ignore the subject.

Malcolm came out with two place settings and

arranged them on the dining table. I moved over to a chair and began eating.

"So…" I poked around with my fork. "What do we do next?"

Malcolm took a deep breath. "I honestly don't know. Maybe wait here for a few years and hope for the best?" I raised an eyebrow at him, and he chuckled. "I joke. But that was what I used to do when something was wrong. It is strange to think I would back down like that. But that was the old me."

I went on. "We are severely outnumbered now. Depending on how the Duchess set up her world, everyone could be on the lookout for us."

"You are right. First I think you need to train a bit more. We need to be at our best before going out. We can't mess up at this point."

Because I already did. I ate some more of my breakfast. "By the way, can you use that power of illusion? I know you said you would be tried for treason if you ever used it in Wonderland and got caught, but what about now?"

He bit his lip. "Well, that is complicated. The rule had nothing to do with the kingdom as much as Wonderland itself. It's sort of like a curse. If I use it, I will automatically die, and I don't think that will change because of the Duchess."

I stared at him. "How did you know it would work in my world?"

Malcolm shrugged. "I didn't in the beginning, but that was before I knew you. I tried it when we went through all the paperwork for the school. Nothing bad happened, so I knew it was fine in your world. Howard was the one who figured it would be fine, and I trusted him. Mainly because he was the one who gave me the curse in the first place."

"Is there a way we can break that curse?"

"Perhaps, but I'd rather not break it. It keeps me in check. Although it would have come in handy right now."

I could understand what he meant. If he had such a strong power, it could corrupt, and by the sounds of it, there was a time in his life where he had too much power. I didn't want him to have to deal with that pain again.

He went on. "So we will train and we will get ready. And what better place to train than here."

I glanced outside as I saw rustling in the bushes. I sighed, knowing he was right. This was the best place to train. It was no wonder he was the strongest fighter in all of Wonderland.

I ran through the Dark Forest—branches and stems of hopefully nothing poisonous scratched at my clothes. Luckily I was able to find some of Davis's old clothes that fit me fine. I could just imagine his face as Chase would harass him about being the same size as me.

My heart ached, thinking back to all the fun times we had.

Those memories were what I was fighting for—those memories would get me through this. I wanted to go back to the way things were, and I would stop at nothing to achieve that. And in order to defeat the Duchess, I first had to be able to defeat Malcolm.

Well, not actually defeat him. I had five minutes to start running and find a hiding spot in the forest, without getting killed by all the creatures in here, until Malcolm would come to find me. The goal was to be able to hide well enough that I could surprise Malcolm by striking first. It was some sick mash-up of tag and hide-and-go-seek, but if I could keep myself hidden from him, then we wouldn't have a problem visiting a town and assessing what the Duchess had changed. Apparently this was how all the others trained when they lived out here. I couldn't help but feel sorry for Davis and Melvin, as I bet Malcolm didn't hold back against them. And it sounded like he was a lot scarier back then.

Malcolm promised I wouldn't get completely lost in the Dark Forest, as if I really tried to get him to find me, he would. I was more afraid of getting attacked by a jabberwocky. Again. Yesterday one decided I looked like a pretty good snack and almost chased me out of the woods. Luckily I was able to collect myself and fight it off just as Malcolm appeared. Let's just say I lost that session of hide-and-seek.

But today was different. I could feel it. I would hide well enough where I could surprise attack him, and he would agree to go to town. It's only been a week of training, yes, but I felt today was my day. And I really just wanted to escape this wretched place even if what was waiting for us on the other side was probably nothing good. I wanted to know, and I wasn't sure I could spend another night worrying about that spider. The day before yesterday, it decided to bring some flowers to apologize to me, but it only made my worry grow. But I had to admit, it was adorable.

I was also starting to get familiar with the layout of the Dark Forest, which surprised me. I was never known to be good at directions, but I supposed since I was in constant fear of getting lost, it was possible for me to finally get good at it.

Passing the cave we stayed in on our first night, I glanced around. It was, in fact, possible to climb over the mouth. Would that be somewhere Malcolm would think to look? Deciding to give it a shot, I made it look like I went inside the cave, then backtracked and climbed above it.

The plan was to wait for Malcolm, have him walk

inside the cave, jump down, and surprise him. He would be most impressed with me, and I could hardly stop smiling. I had finally gotten the better of him. Hopefully.

I could hear the howls of creatures that lived in the Dark Forest. Some of them I didn't even know what they were, and I was too afraid to ask. I figured they were all violent and to just always stay on guard.

After a little while of waiting, Malcolm came into the clearing. I still wasn't sure how he was so good at tracking, as one couldn't see the ground in the Dark Forest since it was covered in fog, but he always showed up around five minutes after I stopped, as if he didn't have to put much effort into looking for me.

I watched as he slowly stepped inside the cave. I grinned as I jumped down as silently as I could. Luckily the ground was covered in moss, so footsteps were almost silent. I placed my hand on the hilt and stepped into the cave behind Malcolm.

He was examining around, trying to see if I was hiding behind one of the rocks. I slowly pulled out my sword so that I could attack.

Well, not actually attack. It would be more of a clumsy half swing without actually touching him. He always said to swing like it was real, as he would always be able to block it, but I didn't feel safe doing that.

I was within five feet of him now, smiling. I had actually won. I couldn't believe it. As I went to tap him with the dull edge of my katana, he quickly turned around and drew his own sword and swung. I blocked it in a swift motion, letting out a high-pitched scream.

Malcolm laughed. "You need to be on guard at all times, Alice. I know you don't like fully swinging, but you have to realize there is no room for hesitation when dealing with an enemy who wants you dead."

"I know…"

"But you did very well to block my attack. I think you are ready. We should head to the nearest town tomorrow."

I jumped up. "Yay!"

"But for the record, I did know you were above the cave. I just wanted to see how well you could try to sneak up on me."

I frowned. I really thought I had gotten the better of him. I should have figured. "But I still passed?"

"Yes, I think you will do fine against the others for now. And I doubt they have the same skills as they did before they were affected by the Duchess."

I wasn't sure if that was a complete compliment or not, but I felt better now that we were finally going to figure out what had happened. "Was Bill easier to go up against when he was affected by Morpheus?"

Malcolm nodded. "A bit. He was still smart and good at tracking, but there was something missing. When you aren't able to think for yourself, you aren't able to use all your skills. At least I don't think so. You become more predictable too."

That made perfect sense. I followed Malcolm as we headed back to his home. I decided it was technically a cottage, as I still hadn't come up with a good name for it. It appeared like a cottage on the inside, especially with all the tea cozies. I collapsed on the couch inside as Malcolm went to the kitchen to make some tea. He did that often, and I wasn't sure if it was something I hadn't noticed, or now that we were back to his home, he was reverting to habits he had while living there. Either way, it was some of the best tasting tea I had ever had.

Malcolm brought out a cup of tea, and I took a sip. It tasted floral with a hint of earthy tones. I set it down and peered up at him.

"So, what town will we be checking out?"

"I am not sure. Everything has been rearranged for the new ruler. I don't even know what the districts are, if there are any different districts. I don't think the Duchess is that creative, so they will more than likely be the same, just arranged a little different."

It was crazy how everything could change like that. I didn't want to think about how much of the Wonderland that I had grown to love had changed.

"If each time Wonderland changes, the districts are changed, then how come the Red and White Kingdom and the Heart Kingdom still existed?"

"Because Alice didn't want them to disappear but left them so we could learn from our mistakes. She also made it impossible for anyone else to change them as well."

I supposed that made sense. It was important to remember the past so one didn't repeat it.

"But I do have a feeling none of the districts except the one she is in will be in good shape. She only cares about herself. I don't remember a day she has ever extended a helping hand, at least not without wanting something in return."

That was definitely clear to me. She used Chase as

her puppet and was willing to hurt my friend in the process. It made sense to me that she wouldn't have cared about anything else.

"But there are parts of Wonderland that can't be changed, or at least I don't think. Well, more things outside the actual borders of Wonderland. We will find out tomorrow. For now, get your rest. Tomorrow is going to be a long day."

I nodded and stretched out a bit. These past few days felt long, but I would finally get my chance to save Kate, if that was even possible.

CHAPTER FOUR

I followed Malcolm through the forest, my hand already on my hilt in case we ran into something, whether they be human or monster. The jabberwocky screamed in the distance. I did not want to face another one of those—I was rather sick of them and couldn't believe how many survived in these woods. I supposed it was better than the bandersnatch. Luckily I hadn't run into one of those again. I did hear their roar every once in a while, however, which left me on edge. The jabberwocky was much easier to take down.

I spotted the singing flowers that encircled the forest and felt much more relieved. It meant that we were almost to the rest of Wonderland and would finally understand what had happened. Although I had been training all week, I didn't know if I was truly prepared. Neither of us had any idea what was waiting for us. For all we knew, they could have the entire Dark Forest surrounded and we were walking into a trap.

But it was better than just sitting around.

We would have to face them sooner or later. What surprised me was that none of them dared go into the Dark Forest after us. I presumed it was because they feared Malcolm and that was his home base, so to speak. He knew that place like the back of his hand, and no one could compare to that.

Except Chase.

It seemed like Chase knew the Dark Forest pretty well. He could have tracked us down just like he tracked Malcolm down when he killed Morpheus. I wondered if he still was the old Chase or if he had been brainwashed again. It didn't seem like he needed to be, as he had been working for the Duchess this entire time.

So there was a possibility of him helping us in the

end.

I wasn't going to expect him to—not after everything that had happened. He had his chances, and yet he never tried to come clean or betray the Duchess, other than when he had said he wanted to run away. That wasn't the same, however, as I wasn't even sure he was trying to escape his fate or that he was actually going to take me straight to the Duchess.

We stepped into the field, and the song of the flowers no longer seemed to affect me. I had grown used to the effects of the Dark Forest, which I wasn't sure was a good thing or not. As we marched forward, Malcolm turned to me.

"After here, we won't know the terrain or what is going on. Be on high alert—even more so than when you are in the Dark Forest. And stay close to me. If anything happens to you, there will be no way to reverse this, and the Duchess knows that. I will protect you no matter the cost. Do you understand?"

I nodded, more worried than I had ever been. What would happen if we ran into any of the others? I would have to fight them, but I didn't know if I could do it. Hopefully it wouldn't come to that, as I had a feeling Malcolm wouldn't hesitate to stop them.

Since I had always focused on not listening to the flowers, I never noticed anything else about them. They were quite beautiful with a rainbow of colors decorating the landscape. It was was similar to how the most beautiful flowers had thorns, except in this case it was a song that would put you to sleep and you would eventually die. I tried not to think about how many people might have met their death there. I figured it wouldn't be too many as they knew to stay away from that place. Even the creatures of the Dark Forest knew to stay away.

They also gave off a pleasant aroma. It smelled of candied apples, grapes, and peaches—like those you would find at a carnival. It reminded me of cotton candy and spending time at the Oregon State Fair. Kate and I had a lot of fun at it last year, of which Chase tagged along and lost all his change on one of the rides, as it flipped us upside down and everything fell out of his pocket. The workers wouldn't let us pick up the change either, which was stupid. They probably were just taking advantage of us because we were teens.

The memory of Chase and Kate and how much fun we had made my heart hurt even more. I had so many great memories with both of them. What if I couldn't move on? What if I really couldn't spend another fun day with them?

What if this was the end?

Noticing my distress, Malcolm grabbed my hand. "It will be okay. Even if we run into trouble, I will get us out of it. Don't worry."

I smiled a little. Although I was worried about what we would find and whether or not we would be captured, I was more hurt due to the fact that everything had come crashing down. "Thank you. I am glad I still have you, but I can't help but think of everything we all have been through. If I had just…"

"It's not your fault. It is the Duchess's and Chase's fault. They are the ones who put you in the position to have to choose between Wonderland and your friend."

I nodded a little, but it didn't help the feeling in my stomach—the feeling saying that I was responsible, that I was the cause of all this. I had betrayed everyone's trust. I had destroyed Wonderland.

No, we would find a way to destroy the Duchess, restore Wonderland, and save Kate. And Chase.

We made it through the flower field and stopped to survey the land. Things appeared normal—large flower fields of the Flower District, stretching as far as the eye could see. The Flower District, although one we always visited since the portal dumped us into a random closet, was rather laid-back and quaint. I found it to be quite beautiful, but it wasn't somewhere most people went unless they had to, which was perfect for us as there would be fewer guards. People traded between lands often, so we could just pretend we were traders.

Despite the fact that the visuals were similar to before the Duchess took over, something about the atmosphere did feel off. Although it was sunny out—a perfect day, in fact—it seemed… fake. It felt like the little town in *Big Fish*, where it was perfect and yet something was most definitely wrong.

This was not good.

I glanced over to Malcolm, who had a frown on his face. He must have felt it too. It wasn't just the fact that we had been in the Dark Forest causing this strange sensation.

"Stay on your guard," Malcolm said. "I have a bad feeling about this."

I nodded as we started forward. In the distance, we could make out the town center or at least where the town center used to be. The silhouette was no longer the same, and I wasn't sure what to expect. It appeared as if there were walls that now surrounded the once open and free town. I gulped, not looking forward to seeing how the place had changed.

I scanned the area for any people roaming around or farmers tending their crops, but there was no one. It was almost as if it had all been abandoned, but by the looks of the crops, it was apparent someone was taking care of them. The more I looked, the more I felt a shiver run down my spine. I didn't like this one bit, but at least there were no guards at the ready to fight us.

We approached the town and found that there was only one point of entry on each side of the now large stone walls that surrounded the place. Before we approached, Malcolm stopped us.

"I don't like seeing this security. It reminds me of when the Queen of Hearts was in charge. However, since no one actually likes the Duchess, I'm hoping it is relaxed and they aren't checking people. Just act like you belong, don't look at them, and walk through without hesitating, all right?"

I nodded. "I got it."

Flipping up our hoods, we headed toward the closest entry point. The guards that stood at the gate didn't seem to be checking anyone, just like Malcolm predicted. I didn't look at him but walked past with Malcolm just as he said. The guard never said anything, and we were in the clear. I let out a sigh as I surveyed the area. My mouth dropped, and I covered it with my hand.

This town used to have beautiful flowers that covered the streets and grew up the buildings, but now everything was plain and appeared almost like that of the industrial revolution. Nothing was beautiful anymore but had grown dirty and full of soot. I couldn't believe my eyes.

I stared at the men and women who once were wearing extraordinary gowns but now wore plain clothes that were worn and dirty. It appeared they hadn't been able to bathe properly in days. I didn't understand how this was possible, as it hadn't been that long. Was this truly the power the Duchess had? Did she really want to have her people living like this?

"It's not polite to stare," Malcolm whispered in my ear.

I turned away from them and looked down at what once used to be the most lush grass that was now hard pavement.

"Why would she do this? Why wouldn't someone

ruling want their citizens to be happy?"

"Because it makes it harder for them to gather resources to rebel."

That made sense. Even in my world this was how dictators took advantage of their people. Was this what it was like everywhere? Was this the hardships they had faced with the Queen of Hearts all those years ago? Most of these people weren't alive, but Malcolm had been. Was this what his life used to be like?

Malcolm went on. "Now come, I want to see if we can get an eye on where she is staying."

I followed Malcolm as we ventured through the town. I tried to keep my eyes away from the people as I felt tears streaming down.

CHAPTER FIVE

This madness went on forever.

We made our way through the town. Some parts of the layout seemed familiar, other parts of it did not. We headed forward, however, as we were just trying to get through it so we could head toward the Duchess's mansion. I recognized cafés and some businesses, but ones that had been on the other side of the city were now located where we walked. It was utter madness. Nothing seemed right.

No one seemed to pay us much mind as we ventured through, mingling with traders and such. There were vendors who were selling flowers, which were still beautiful as they had been when we'd passed the fields, but the sellers didn't look too happy to be there. Not many seemed to be purchasing flowers either, which was concerning.

It didn't matter. I would fix this. They wouldn't have to suffer much longer.

I still couldn't believe that only a week had passed. Was this really the same Wonderland? Did they know only that much time had gone by, or did this erase their memories of earlier and they believed they had lived their entire lives like this? How would this affect my world as all the citizens were dreams?

"I still can't believe this is happening," I whispered to Malcolm. "I wish I had known—"

"What the Duchess did is not your fault. She could have easily taken over and been a benevolent leader. As I said earlier, this is what it was like when the Queen of Hearts ruled. My guess is she wants to rule just like her —with fear in everyone's eyes," Malcolm explained.

I shook my head. "I just don't understand. This used to be such a beautiful place. Who would want this?"

"Monsters, that's who. She knew that no one would obey her rule, so she made it so they couldn't do anything to revolt. I've seen it all before. Now let's see what shape the capital is in and if that is where she is ruling all of this. If I had to guess, her mansion is where the capital palace once was."

I nodded and followed him as we left this dreary city behind.

The road from the Flower District to the capital wasn't too long, if it was the same layout. We would have to go through some woods and prairies, but that wasn't difficult. It was mostly flat, and I wouldn't have to climb. I hated elevation changes, more for going down as it always made my knees feel unstable.

There weren't many people on the roads—just a trader here and there. They nodded to us and said hello, but that was it. We kept our heads down when we came across them and waved. They didn't seem to care, so our original notion of everyone being on the lookout for us had been wrong. Perhaps the Duchess didn't have as much power as we had originally thought.

The forest felt like walking through the redwoods in southern Oregon. We had explored these woods many times in the couple of years I had been coming to

Wonderland. They were rather magical and beautiful. I could spend days out here, painting every scenery I found. I was glad they were still in the same shape as they had been before the change. It would have been sad to see such beautiful places disappear.

Glancing at Malcolm, I found him surveying the land as we moved, as if on the lookout. We were wearing hooded capes, but it wouldn't be enough if we found someone looking for us or we ran into Melvin and the others. I gulped, praying that we wouldn't be spotted or have to face them. If we were captured, I didn't know if there would be any way out of this. I had been captured before a couple of times, but this time there wouldn't be anyone to save us. This time it would be the end.

No, I couldn't think like that. I had to stay positive. Just because there were only two of us didn't mean that we wouldn't win. Malcolm would come up with something, and I would go along with it. It was my fault we were in this mess, and I wouldn't argue with Malcolm ever again.

Because my friend still died.

I held back the tears, not wanting to have a complete breakdown in the middle of the path. We would figure out a way to save her—I just knew it.

We made it to the capital, and I couldn't believe my eyes. What was once an intricate and artistic city was now a walled-off manor, similar to the one we'd visited. The more I looked at it, the more I realized it was the same building. Malcolm had been right.

"How…," I began.

"She used your magic spell to move where her mansion was. She must have still wanted it. It is a gorgeous building, to be honest. Just a horrible host."

I nodded. That made sense, as the kingdoms changed. "So the old capital is gone?"

"Seems so. Which is odd…"

"What do you mean?"

Malcolm didn't answer my question but narrowed his eyes at the horizon. He stopped walking, as if searching for something. I stopped as well, not wanting to go any farther into that mess. I saw the familiar nicely cut hedges, the gorgeous roses, water fountains as far as the eye could see. Money didn't seem to be a big deal in this world, but that didn't mean she wasn't guilty living like this and forcing all the citizens into poverty. It just wasn't right.

"What are we going to do now?"

He pursed his lips. "I definitely don't think we should

go any farther. I just wanted to see what we were up against."

That made sense. I turned back to the mansion. I wondered if Chase was in there, still serving the Duchess like he always had been. As for the rest, were they still alive? Were they brainwashed into being her guard, just like what Morpheus did? I had a feeling that was the case as the Duchess would want strong people on her side to protect her from us.

Malcolm glanced around again. "Let's head back. I don't like being out here for any longer than we already have."

I nodded. "Agreed. And I don't think we will want to stay outside the Dark Forest for the night."

"No, we won't. Luckily we are on the side of the Dark Forest that is closer to my cottage. I just figured searching for the Flower District would be the safest thing to do first." He peered over at the mansion. "And I also wanted to see this place with my own eyes."

I agreed—now seeing this place made our situation all the more real. We had to do something before it was too late, but how? Hopefully we could come up with a plan soon. More than likely, it would have to do with killing the Duchess.

As we began to head toward the Dark Forest, Malcolm abruptly stopped and held his hand out. "Stay close to me."

My heart raced as I heard footsteps behind me. I got closer to Malcolm and prayed it was someone just passing by.

"Hey! You two! Stop!"

I knew that voice. It was Bill. I heard Malcolm curse under his breath. I glanced back to find it was just Bill on a horse—there were no signs of the others.

"What are you two doing on the outskirts of the capital?"

Malcolm kept his head down, as not to reveal his face. "We were simply looking for places to work. We didn't realize we were on the road to the capital."

"Oh? And what citizen doesn't know where the capital is?"

"A very turned-around lost one. But since we were mistaken, we are heading back now. Thank you for keeping our country safe." Malcolm grabbed my hand and started forward toward the forest.

"Did you really think I would fall for that, Malcolm and Alice?" He laughed. "Now turn yourselves in before I use force."

"Run! Remember last time!" Malcolm exclaimed as he pushed me forward. I began to run when I realized Malcolm wasn't following. I turned around to find him drawing his sword. No, he wasn't going to do that to me again. If I helped him, we would outnumber Bill. Between the two of us, we could take him down.

But I couldn't clash swords with Bill as I would never want to deal the final blow. I could, however, distract him long enough to let Malcolm knock him out.

I glanced around for anything that I could truly distract someone like Bill with. I bit my lip. What would distract Bill? Then it hit me as he jumped off the horse.

I put my hands around my mouth and shouted. "Oh hey, Kenny! What are you doing over there?"

Bill spun around to see what mess Kenny was getting into but found I was lying. Malcolm picked up on what I had done and used the butt of his sword to knock Bill out. Grabbing his horse, Malcolm led it to where I was waiting.

"I told you to run." He tried to seem mad at me, but I could see the smile trying to appear on his lips.

"Yeah, well, I wasn't going back to the Dark Forest on my own, so I figured I would help."

Malcolm helped me on the horse and mounted as well. With a slight kick, we headed back toward the Dark Forest.

"You could have gotten captured pulling that stunt." He apparently wasn't letting this go.

"But I didn't, and I figured you could use some help. Not to sound like a damsel in distress, but I really don't think I could take down the Duchess by myself. There are too many people after me—people who I recognize are stronger than me. Which is why I will always try to think of easy ways to de-escalate the situation."

"Like yelling 'Hey, Kenny'?"

I nodded. "Yup. Admit it, it was clever and kind of funny if not for the fact we almost got arrested."

"It was, but he's going to have one heck of a headache when he wakes up, not to mention be mad about his horse."

"Speaking of which, what are we going to do about the horse once we get to the Dark Forest?"

"We will let it go. The military horses we have are quite smart and always head back to the capital once set free. Sometimes even when you don't want them to, leaving you stranded and having to walk all the way back."

I smiled as I could imagine a horse doing that. We set forward and prayed that we wouldn't run into any of the others.

CHAPTER SIX

We jumped off the horse, and Malcolm whistled at him. He abruptly turned and sauntered off, as if that was the cue to go home, or perhaps he didn't want to be near the Dark Forest any longer than he had to. I didn't blame him.

Malcolm turned to me. "Well, ready to go back home?"

He used the word *home* ironically, as he knew I didn't want to be back in the Dark Forest. I rolled my eyes as we stepped through the singing flowers.

It was nice having time with Malcolm after we had

spent quite a few months ignoring each other. It was also nice to see him in good spirits, given that fact that Wonderland was now controlled by a ruthless madwoman. It meant he had hope, and if he had hope, then so did I.

I didn't like the fact I felt so helpless right now, not to mention anxiety randomly overtaking me at any moment. What was I supposed to do when it felt like there was nothing I could do. I had the entire world shatter before me, and it was my fault.

Grabbing my hand, Malcolm squeezed it. How he always knew when I was distraught, I wasn't sure, but it was comforting to know that he was there for me when I needed him most. I just had to make sure to be there for him and the others.

I would save them all if it was the last thing I did.

We reached the denser part of the Dark Forest, past the singing flowers, and I was welcomed back by the roars of the jabberwocky. I sighed as we moved forward, which made Malcolm laugh a little. I was getting used to the sounds, but they still made the hair on the back of my neck raise a bit. I couldn't wait to get out of there again.

"So what are we going to do next?" I asked as we

crouched under some thick branches.

Malcolm let out a sigh. "I'm working on it. I am playing all the possibilities in my head and going through everything I know about Wonderland and determining what our safest plan of action can be."

I nodded. "Safest, huh? Is there really a safe plan?"

"I hope so."

That made me chuckle in the way one laughs when there was nothing else they could do. I didn't know Wonderland like Malcolm did, so I doubted I could come up with the best solution; however, sometimes a newcomer could bring different eyes to the table and solve a problem in a way no one else thought of.

So I began to let my mind wander about what I did know about Wonderland. I knew that there were different eras and that the old kingdoms were still standing, although no one went there anymore. I knew that Chase would look there first for us, so it wouldn't be a good hiding spot long term. I knew since the mansion was where the king and queen once lived, that it was likely they had been erased from this era. I knew if Chase's memories were altered, that he would be the only person we could convince to help us. However, no one in the Flower District seemed to care that we were walking around. Even if they didn't see us under our hoods, one would think that the guards would check everyone coming in and out of the town.

Which meant she had less control over everyone than we realized.

"Do you think the Duchess focused more on those with roles than the dreams in this world? Since they would be the most powerful to take her down. Then she just made living hard for everyone else so they couldn't use resources to fight her."

Malcolm glanced at me. "That makes sense. It seemed odd that none of the guards stopped us. Perhaps we can trust certain people after all then. However, I don't want to lower my guard, as we can't have any screwups."

That was fair. But it was something we could potentially use. I smiled, satisfied that I deduced something. Now I just needed to figure out how to use it to solve my problem.

It occurred to me that we didn't really know anyone outside our circle. "Why don't you guys befriend people outside your circle? I mean, besides because you were in my world a lot. But it doesn't seem like you interact much."

Malcolm shrugged as he moved some hanging moss out of the way to walk under. "It's not that we don't want to interact with them, but more… that they don't stick around."

"Ah. I guess I never thought of that."

"We are much older than all of them, and we will continue living after they are gone. It's hard to make connections. So typically those with roles stick together."

"But that would make broken friendships even that much harder, I bet."

He nodded. "Yes it does. You hold grudges and learn whether or not someone is worthy of trusting again. Take Chase for example. It had been decades since he said he broke ties with the Duchess, but I never believed because I knew he was a liar. And I was right."

I realized I shouldn't have brought it up. I let out a breath. Their fight never seemed to end. However, now I understood what type of betrayals would cause such strife between two people. It made sense that he wouldn't trust him, as I doubted I could ever trust Chase again.

We made it back to the cottage, and I double-checked

the couch for the spider before collapsing on it. My body started shaking as I realized what had happened— we had almost been captured by Bill, and the past week of training would have been for nothing.

"Are we going to be able to do this?" I peered over at Malcolm as he hung up his cloak. He looked at me with sad eyes for a moment, then turned to the kitchen.

"I'm going to make us some tea."

I closed my eyes and rubbed my face as he went into the kitchen. It was clear Bill had been brainwashed, but at least his love for Kenny hadn't changed and I was able to use that to our advantage. But it all was still concerning.

How were we going to get past them in order to take down the Duchess?

I thought back to how the citizens didn't seem to be brainwashed like Bill was. Did that mean Zachariah and Penny remembered who we were? They and their daughter were the only people I had really gotten to know here in Wonderland. Would they turn us in if they recognized us? Or would they help?

The problem was they had no skill in fighting, and I wouldn't want anything bad to happen to them if they helped us. So it was out of the question to talk to them.

Besides, Chase knew of their existence and was probably keeping an eye on their home.

"Here you go." Malcolm stepped into the room. I opened my eyes to find him holding two cups of tea with a smile. I sat up as he handed one to me.

"Thank you." I blew on it some and took a sip. It was a mix of berry, black, and green tea with a hint of rose. It was one of my favorite blends he had. It was sweet yet hearty. I could drink it every day and not get sick of it.

He took a seat across from me. "Now, to answer your question, I don't think just the two of us will be able to take down the Duchess by ourselves. Not after seeing what we saw."

I frowned. I didn't think he would be so upfront about his thoughts. He wasn't one to say something was impossible unless it really was. What did that mean for us?

"What are we going to do then? I don't particularly want to live here for an eternity, not to mention they will eventually come out here for us."

"That is true. I give it about a month before they try, but they will have a good plan by then. I doubt we would win, even on my own turf."

Well, at least I wouldn't have to be out there for that long. I gulped, waiting for him to go on.

"But I think there is a way for us to win. The problem is, we will have to find Dodo."

Like the one in the caucus race. I knew that there were other characters in the novel, but I never asked about them in case it brought up bad memories, like Howard.

"And what is wrong with that?" I asked. "I mean, if you think it is possible. And why wouldn't he have been affected by the change?"

"Well, Dodo gave up on being involved with Wonderland affairs and now lives outside the boundaries. So, therefore, he isn't affected by anything that is happening within Wonderland."

"Well, that's good news for us. Why don't we go now?"

He let out a sigh and set down his tea. It was never a good sign when he set down his tea. "The problem is that Dodo… He always asks a price for whatever he helps with. We have to be willing to give up whatever he asks."

That didn't seem like a big deal, given the circumstances. "I'll do anything. Wonderland will be destroyed at this rate, not to mention the Duchess wants me killed anyway."

"There's another thing."

How could there be more? It seemed like nothing could get more complicated than it already was, but Wonderland always seemed to like to surprise me. "What is it?"

"He… he might be able to bring back Kate."

I couldn't believe what I was hearing. This entire time, he knew of a way to bring back my best friend? Why hadn't he said anything earlier?"I'll do whatever he asks."

"He could ask for your life in exchange. Or my life, or maybe even Wonderland. You can never tell with him."

But could he really be any worse than the Duchess? I shook my head. "There is only one way to find out. Let's go find him."

"So why don't we just head toward where the Dodo is? I mean, if he isn't within the boundaries of Wonderland, then he shouldn't have been moved in the change, right?" I asked as I watched Malcolm pace back and forth. We had made a decision the night before that we would visit the Dodo, but after that, Malcolm seemed to be deep in thought, as if there was more to this than he was letting on.

Malcolm stopped pacing and took a sip of his tea.

Today it was an Earl Grey-tasting tea. Setting the cup down, he glanced over at me. "Although he hasn't changed locations, I'm not completely sure which direction to head."

I furrowed my eyebrows. Malcolm was supposedly the greatest tracker in all of Wonderland. How would he not know how to find someone? "Wouldn't north, south, and all that be the same?"

He shook his head. "When we went out yesterday, the sun rose and set in different spots compared to normal. The Duchess did a real number in regard to knowing which was north and south. I was able to orient myself so I could find the Dark Forest fine, but to find the Dodo, we will need a map. He isn't someone I visited regularly, not to mention he could have moved. But with a map, I might be able to deduce where he is and which way to head."

I leaned farther back into the couch and clutched a pillow against my chest. Why was everything always harder than it needed to be in this place? Why couldn't we just be able to find someone easily?

"Not only that, but since Bill found us, I'm afraid they are going to heighten security, not to mention someone might figure out we will go to the edges for help. I doubt anyone would side with her, since they all know how corrupt she is, and they have more power on the outside so she won't dare cross them. But she might have rearranged the edges so he and a few others will be hard to find for us."

"What others? Is there anyone else we can find? Maybe we can gather them all and they can help us."

Malcolm shrugged. "We can, but I know they won't help at all. Dodo is the only one with power and knowledge of Wonderland that we can use. It's crazy, but he is said to be older than time itself."

It wasn't the strangest thing I had heard, but it was definitely up there. "You're right. That is crazy."

Malcolm let out a chuckle to my comment and rubbed his forehead with his hand. "He was also Howard's mentor and taught him everything he knew. Since he knew Howard, I'm hoping he will help us."

I sipped my tea, thinking back about Howard. I hadn't known him that long, but from what I could tell, he seemed like a pretty nice guy. He was Malcolm's mentor and was wiser than anyone else I'd known. Having witnessed his death, I clutched the pillow even more, trying to rid myself of those images. I could only imagine how Malcolm felt as he was standing closer to him.

But if he'd taught Howard, then he had to be wise and willing to help us. Then again, Count Dooku taught Qui-Gon Jinn.

"Have you ever meet Dodo?"

Malcolm hesitated. "Well, sort of. It was while I was the executioner. He might have been on a list. But he survived. One of the few that did. He was saved by Alice, actually."

So he was supposed to kill him but didn't only because of Alice. That was a great start. "Ah."

He smiled. "But I'm hoping since you are with me, he will listen. And because I worked with Howard. And because it's been a few centuries… I'm hopeful. Although some people do hold grudges against others in Wonderland, most people get over things after a while. If everyone were to hold grudges, then no one would like me, if I were honest."

Sort of like how no one liked Chase. Then again, all their suspicions were correct. I let out a sigh. "Well, hopefully he's forgiven you. Or he listens because I am there."

"Exactly. And although you aren't the same Alice, the old Alice did save him, so he owes her. He's never one to forget a debt."

"Which means he might not ask for something in return because of that debt, doesn't it?"

He shrugged. "It depends what he thinks is of equal value. But yes, you do have a point. But there is still a chance he will ask for something in return, especially if we are asking more than one thing of him. Hopefully it isn't something too horrible. Unless it's the Duchess's head. I could work with that."

I didn't know how to answer that. After everything that had happened in Wonderland, I still didn't believe violence was the answer unless truly necessary. But right now it felt necessary to have to kill her. I just wished the king and queen could have succeeded in ending her life before Chase messed it all up. Before Kate was teleported there and vanished.

I pushed back the thought of my best friend. "So what should we do now?"

Malcolm let out a long breath. "Well, we need to go back into town to get a map. However, when a change happens, everyone automatically knows where things are, within reason. They at least have a concept of where all the lands are."

"So if we ask, there is a possibility that they will

realize we weren't part of the change and that we are wanted."

"Exactly. Not to mention maps aren't in great demand. People do need them to plan routes and such, just in case someone gets lost. But other than that, there aren't many sold."

"So asking around where to get a map and then buying the map will both seem suspicious?"

He nodded. "Yup. So we will need a plan on what to say to not seem odd."

I bit my lip, thinking of excuses that seemed reasonable. We couldn't just say we were lost nor that we were on a journey as it seemed that many didn't journey. We couldn't pretend to be traders as we didn't have any goods on us.

Then it hit me.

"What if we say we are looking for work in the districts due to how poor everything is and we need a map that lays out the districts so we can mark them off?" I asked.

Malcolm took a sip of tea. "That's not a bad idea. It would definitely be a good idea and wouldn't be out of the ordinary. Although, no matter the excuse, it could be possible that everyone who asks about maps is checked out and interrogated."

That was a big possibility. "So should we just sneak in and steal one?"

"That would probably just get us arrested. I think your first plan would be all right and hope that they haven't sent out word that we were spotted yet. The guards in the Flower District didn't seem to care that we walked in, so we should try there again."

I nodded. "That makes sense. Even if they had been given the orders, perhaps since they have been treated so poorly, they will just ignore them and not care we waltz in all over again."

"Precisely. But we should still come up with a backup plan in case they attack."

I sighed. "Are you saying I will have to go hide in the forest again?"

Malcolm chuckled. "No, but perhaps we do some sprints later today just to warm up in case something does happen. And we should come up with a meetup area."

"But in order to make a meetup area, we will need a map."

Malcolm gave me a look, and I smiled. "But seriously, we aren't one hundred percent sure with the layout, and so a meetup area might not be as easy as that. I'm getting better at directions, but that doesn't mean I would be able to find something."

"Well, what if the meetup area was here?"

I wrinkled my nose. "But then I would have to go through the Dark Forest on my own."

"You are getting better at knowing the layout of this area. No guard would follow you in here."

He had a point there. Even most of the others wouldn't follow us in there, which is why they hadn't come searching yet. "But what if it was Bill or Melvin or something?"

"Well…" He took a sip of tea. "Let's just hope that it isn't."

I put my finger to my chin. "What if we made the meetup spot be somewhere we pick along the way outside the Dark Forest but close enough so that if we need to get anyone off our tail, we could? We can mark it with some nondescript paint or something; and then we will know which spot it is and hopefully I will remember where it is."

Malcolm nodded. "That could work. Just hopefully you remember."

I gave him an innocent smile. "I'm getting better, I

swear!"

A smile appeared on the edge of his lips. "So you say. But hopefully it won't come to that. We should be able to stick together the entire time."

"Right. But a backup plan is always nice to have. Is there anything else we need to think of?"

Malcolm shook his head. "Nothing we need to do until we get the map. We might need some gear to camp with, but that will make our journeying to find work story appear even more real."

"Right then." I took a sip of the tea. "Shall we train?"

CHAPTER EIGHT

Malcolm made me wear a cloak again. It didn't really make us blend in. In fact, we stood out more as it was kind of warm and no one else was wearing a jacket. It was obvious we were trying to be inconspicuous.

Everyone always tried wearing a hood and cloak to hide who they really were, but I always thought that made them stand out even more. However, a lot of people knew our faces, or at least a good chunk of them did, so we couldn't exactly move around without something to shadow our faces. Either way, it was like we were walking around with a target painted on ourselves. Or maybe like a neon blinking sign that said Here They Are.

As we approached the town, I let out a slight sigh. Seeing the once beautiful Flower District now surrounded by walls and the beautiful plants now ruined made my heart ache. This place, once the circus had been destroyed, was always open and full of magic. Now it felt like something out of industrial Europe or even the Middle Ages, except more advanced. But the feeling of exclusion and defense was there, which was not something I was used to in Wonderland. The original story, yes, but not the Wonderland I had gotten to know and love.

I turned to Malcolm. "Too bad you can't use that illusion magic. It would really come in handy right about now."

Malcolm let out a small laugh. "Wouldn't that have been convenient? But that is not the case, and I will more than likely never get to use it again."

I felt a little bad for bringing it up, but I didn't like the quiet as we made our way to the town. It made me even more nervous. After what happened just a couple of days before, I was afraid they were waiting for us this time and it would be the end.

Malcolm took my hand. "But we won't need it. I am confident this will work and we will be able to restore Wonderland."

I smiled a little and nodded. "Yeah. And save our friends."

"Of course. And teach that cat a lesson or two about loyalty."

I didn't want to think about Chase anymore, but I couldn't help it. What had he gone through all these years? What would have happened if he had told us the truth? If Wonderland was full of curses, perhaps he had one too.

We stopped on the road a little ways away from the entrance to the town. Malcolm turned to me. "Are you ready?"

I took a deep breath. "As ready as I will ever be. We will be quick and get going before it is too late. I'm ready to do this."

"That's my Alice."

We stepped forward toward the entrance, and I prayed that we would be able to find a map easily. Were there map stores? Were there tourist stores that sold maps and things like that? I never had to buy a map before since I was always with Malcolm or Chase and they knew their way around. But now that the Duchess changed things up a bit, although she wasn't too creative with the new districts, I could tell some layouts were different. It was enough to confuse us, which was probably the smartest way to baffle one's enemy—have it look the same but a little different in order to disorient someone. I noted a building that was on the opposite side of town before the switch. If I hadn't been paying attention, I would have thought I was entering from the wrong direction.

"So, where would one find a map?"

Malcolm shrugged. "I have no idea. I haven't needed one other than to draw out military strategies, but we are given those in the capital…" He tapped his chin. "We could…"

"I think sneaking into a military area should be the last place we look."

He gestured with his arms. "Fine. Where do you suggest we look first?"

I thought about it for a moment. If I were in my world, walking around a town, where would the first place I look be? Then it hit me.

"What about going into a pub or restaurant and asking them if there is somewhere we can find a map? Wouldn't that be the first place travelers go in a new area? As they need to get food and water?"

He smiled. "Great idea. Let's do that."

Malcolm and I made our way to the first restaurant we found. It was a mix of a pub and diner. Luckily, as some pubs in Oregon didn't allow minors, this one did as Wonderland didn't have the same laws. I glanced around to find the area to be clean, although a little worn down from the change. It was quiet and decent enough. It also wasn't noon yet, so there were very few people inside.

"Take a seat anywhere you like!" the bartender called out as we entered. Malcolm and I nodded, and we took a spot in the back where it was darker and out of the way.

"Are you hungry? Because I'm not really…," I whispered.

"We can order some snacks to at least fit in." He scanned the menu. "It doesn't seem that they have any good tea."

"Well, it is a pub."

He sighed. "It's because of the Duchess though.

When Alice made the Dream Kingdom, she made it so everywhere had tea. The Duchess would have specifically taken that out. It's fine. I'll just have water."

I didn't know whether to laugh a little or feel bad. I did feel a little bit of jealousy at the original Alice as she had done that for Malcolm. I wondered if he still liked her or if his feelings had left and she was just another person from his past.

No, it didn't matter. He and I were together now, and that was all that mattered.

After a bit, a waitress came over to get our order. She appeared the same age as me but had bags under her eyes, and her hair, although clean, was rather frizzed out as if she had dealt with a lot in the past few days. "What would you two like to order?"

"I would like an order of fries," I answered with a smile.

"And we will share that," Malcolm added. "And a couple of waters."

The waitress jotted it down. "Coming right up." She spun around and headed for the bar.

After she left, I realized something. "Wait, do we have money?"

Malcolm nodded. "I have some I always keep on me. Hopefully it is the same currency this time around. I doubt that would have changed, but one never knows with the Duchess. I mean, she even got rid of good tea just to be inconvenient to me."

"So it's possible that she changed the currency."

He shrugged. "Yeah. But I honestly doubt it will matter. Besides, the moment we ask about a map, they already are going to be suspicious of us. We will just put the money down and let her keep the change. It would be the best option."

"But we will have to pay for the map."

"That is true. Let's just hope the currency is the same."

I nodded. A little bit later, the waitress came back with our fries. They had been freshly cooked and were still very hot, but I put one in my mouth like an idiot anyway.

"Would you like anything else?" she asked.

Malcolm answered as I was dealing with my hot fry issue. "We were wondering where we could find a map of the land. We have been traveling and wanted a map so we could mark off the places we tried for work. Seems most places aren't hiring."

She seemed hesitant for a moment and then smiled. "There is a shop down the street that should have a map or two available. Not many travel far, after the change." She let out a sigh. "No one can afford it."

Malcolm glanced over at me and noticed the worry on my face. I couldn't help but to fret about these people—it was my fault they were going through with this. We had to succeed. I couldn't watch these people suffer anymore.

Malcolm smiled at her. "Thank you. Your information is much appreciated."

We finished up our fries, which were some of the best fries I had ever eaten—even better than McMenamins, which was a pub chain in the Northwest. They had some great burgers as well. I wasn't sure how the rest of the food was on the menu and was surprised that the fries here were so good. Then again, I had been eating random things Malcolm had made from the Dark Forest, and many of them weren't that tasty. This might have just seemed good because of that. I would have to come back later, just to check.

After the waitress brought us our bill, Malcolm set some money down and we hurried out of the pub before they could see what currency we paid with. The shop the waitress mentioned wasn't too far away—within sight of the pub. Malcolm led us across the street. I couldn't help but look down at the pavement, missing the grass that once made up the roads.

As we entered the building, something seemed off. There were only two others in the shop, browsing around. It almost felt like in movies where something bad was going to happen but the main characters didn't quite know it yet. I glanced over to Malcolm, who was peering around as if looking for something.

He felt it too—something was very off about all this. I watched as the people inside eyed us. Did they know? My heart started to race, but we needed the map, and if they knew who we were, it was too late to turn around.

Malcolm stepped up to the cashier. "Do you sell maps?"

The man gulped and nodded. "Yeah, I have one right here." He handed it to Malcolm.

"How much do they cost?"

The man, who fiddled with his collar, shrugged. "On the house. Not many ask for maps these days. I'm just trying to get rid of them."

Malcolm nodded. "Thank you." He turned to me and gently grabbed my wrist while whispering in my ear.

"We need to run. Once we get outside, start for where we promised to meet up."

My heart raced even more. So there was something wrong. I had been right. Malcolm and I stepped outside, and I began running toward the entrance of the district.

CHAPTER NINE

As we stepped outside the shop, a handful of guards were approaching. Malcolm squeezed my hand even tighter.

"This is not good."

"You two! Put your hands up!" a soldier warned as he pulled out his sword.

I gulped. At least it wasn't a gun as I could fight him off with my own sword.

Which also meant I didn't need to raise my hands

quite yet.

"The ones on the right look less experienced. If we run at them, they won't know what to do."

I nodded as we both started running at them. Just as Malcolm predicted, they didn't know what to do and we were able to make it past them.

The first guard called out after us. "Stop them!"

Lucky for us, it didn't seem that any of the citizens seemed to care about wanting to help. We pushed past them, and they didn't bother to even try to stop us, which was good for us. I wondered if it was because they were confused about what was going on or if it was because they knew we might be able to stop the Duchess.

I peered back to find all the guards running after us— their swords in hand. My eyes widened.

"Don't look back! Just keep running!" Malcolm said as he kept his hand intertwined with mine, leading me through the maze that was this district. I couldn't help but to look back as I wanted to know what was after us.

"How did they know where we were?"

"They probably knew we would need a map and waited in all the districts for someone asking around. It couldn't be helped."

"What are we going to do now?"

"Keep running of course."

I did just that as we made our way through the city. We headed straight for the exit but found that the guards had already blocked it. There were at least five of them waiting with their swords drawn. Malcolm cursed under his breath and turned us down a different path.

"How are we going to get out of here?" I asked as we kept on running.

"I'm working on that. This is why I hate walls so much."

I thought back to all the movies and shows that I had seen and couldn't come up with anything other than jumping the wall, which seemed impossible. I glanced up at the wall and the roofs. Was it possible? Would this become an *Assassin's Creed* game? I wasn't sure, but I had to point it out.

"Can we get on any of these roofs? Then maybe we can jump…"

He glanced up and sort of made a shrug, as if considering. "That could work… Problem is, we will need to get up to the roof. Keep your eyes open for any ladders or stairs that they can't get the advantage over us with."

I nodded as we started searching as we ran. I doubted even any of those buildings had access to the roofs from the inside, so odds were they needed to have some kind of access on the outside. So far, there was nothing. Perhaps they put away their ladders when they were done with them.

The soldiers yelled after us, but they were a lot slower than we were. It was a good idea that we trained so hard in the Dark Forest as running through these streets was a lot easier than through the forest. People seemed to get out of the way as we ran as well, which helped. I felt the guards would have stopped and scolded them if it weren't for the fact that they needed to keep running after us.

Lucky for us, we didn't have to deal with the guards getting ahead of us and surrounding us like they did in movies since none of them listened to each other. As I glanced back, I could see the frustration on what I would assume was the leader's face. They were not used to this.

Then it hit me. It was because there hadn't been any enemy they had to fight against in Wonderland for quite some time.

Sure there were guards before the change, but within the districts, it was pretty laid-back. They didn't have to chase anyone, I wouldn't think, as general crime was pretty low. The only people who did that were those who served the capital—mainly those who served under Bill.

So we had the advantage.

We rounded a corner and found that it was a dead end. Luckily, however, there was a ladder against one of the buildings. This was our only chance.

"Up the ladder. Now!" Malcolm ordered. I hurried up, careful not to look down as I still wasn't quite used to heights and still hated them with a passion. Fortunately I am able to push past my fears and keep going. That, and because if I stopped I would be arrested. If that wasn't a motivator, I wasn't sure what was.

I noticed that Malcolm wasn't right behind me, and I peered down, which was a mistake, and saw he had his sword drawn, ready to fight off the guards.

"Malcolm!"

"Keep going! I will meet you up there, I promise!"

I looked up again and then back to Malcolm. It didn't seem right to have him fight all those guards by himself, but I had learned not to disobey his order. Then a plan hit me, and thankfully I had been working on my upper arm and core strength.

Hurrying up the ladder, I looked down to find the guards all surrounding Malcolm. The first one slashed at Malcolm, but he was able to counter and push him back.

"Malcolm!" I exclaimed. "Grab the ladder!"

He glanced up, then smiled when he realized what I was about to do. He quickly swung forward to make the guards back up and then grabbed on. With all my strength, I pulled up the ladder as fast as I could. Malcolm held on as he flew through the air and toward the roof. The guards tried to reach for the ladder before it was raised all the way up to the roof but failed.

Malcolm stood up on the roof.

"Grab the ladder. We can use it to get down the wall."

I nodded and helped him carry it as we hurried toward the wall. The building we were on was close to the wall so we wouldn't have to jump roof to roof. There was the issue, however, of getting to the wall from the roof.

We got to the edge of the building and peered down

to find the guards following, but they couldn't do anything to get to us. I had a feeling that some of them probably went to go get some ladders.

"We can walk across the ladder to get to the other side. It isn't that long, and this is pretty sturdy wood."

My eyes widened. "You can't be serious."

"It will be fine. I promise."

I sighed and mumbled, "Kids, don't try this at home."

Malcolm dropped the ladder over to the wall and ran across it like it was no big deal. I stared at it and gulped. As I glanced down, I found that one of the guards had found a ladder.

Taking in a deep breath and using my core to hold me up just like Becca taught me in dance, I ran across the ladder. Malcolm caught me before I could run off the edge of the wall.

"Whoa there. You made it. Breathe."

I nodded quickly, and Malcolm grabbed the ladder and put it on the other side of the wall. There were no guards below us, but there were some citizens. They didn't seem to notice us standing on the top of the wall.

We placed the ladder down on the opposite side before the guards could use their ladder to climb the wall. We slid down it as fast as we could, which was terrifying and not something I would ever recommend. Luckily, the wood was slick and I didn't get any splinters along the way. Malcolm knocked the ladder over as we glanced around, trying to figure out where we should go next.

The problem with the Flower District was that it was surrounded by fields, so no matter which direction we ran, they would see us. That is, unless we ran around the walls so they wouldn't see which way we disappeared to.

I grabbed Malcolm's hand. "Come on, this way."

He grinned a little as he usually took the initiative. I was getting better at leading, and for that I was happy. But I couldn't use this time to pat myself on the back.

The guards shouted at us, but we ignored them. I glanced back and found they had decided to try to get down from the wall before pursuing us, which was good for us as we had a little time before they could get down with the ladder. Hopefully we could disappear without them knowing which way we went.

As we rounded the corner, I heard someone call out my name.

"Alice, is that you?"

I peered around to find Zachariah sitting on his

wagon. With a swift motion, Malcolm pulled out his sword and pointed it at him. I quickly grabbed his arm.

"No, he is a friend."

"It doesn't matter anymore. Everyone is the enemy."

Zachariah shook his head. "No, my family wasn't affected like the others. We don't have a drive to hurt either of you. Now hurry—get into the wagon and I can take you back to the house before they notice where you have gone."

I glanced over at Malcolm, who seemed hesitant. "I trust him."

Malcolm narrowed his eyes but heard the guards were getting closer to finding us, their shouts coming from around the corner "Fine. Let's get in."

We got in and ducked underneath some of the cloth just as the soldiers came pouring out of the entrance. The cloth covered some fruit and hay, which made my allergies start acting up, but I did my best to keep from sneezing. Malcolm peered out from under the sheet as Zachariah ordered his horse to move forward.

"They don't seem to know where we went but don't seem suspicious of everyone. I think we are in the clear."

I let out a breath. Hopefully we would be out of sight

soon and I could get out from under this cloth and sneeze to my heart's content.

CHAPTER TEN

After a while, when we were in the clear, Malcolm and I were able to come out from under the covering and sit near the front of the wagon. Malcolm kept his eyes out for behind us, but I looked forward toward Zachariah.

"So, Zachariah… Uh… How have you been?" I asked and immediately wished I hadn't. It was a stupid question as it was clear that all of Wonderland was suffering.

"All things considered, the three of us are hanging in there just fine. The district main towns were what were affected the most. It seems the Duchess didn't think us farm folk were of much worry."

So he did understand what was going on. I knew I could trust Zachariah. "So none of the farmers were affected in that they want to hurt me?"

He shook his head. "No, we all agreed if we saw you, we would help. We want the old Wonderland restored. I'm not sure if anyone would put their necks on the line… but they wouldn't turn you in. So as long as it isn't guards who see you out here, you are fine."

I nodded. It was good to hear that not everyone had given up on me, but I knew this was all my fault. I would make it right, however, and all this pain would be erased.

Malcolm didn't say anything as we made our way through the farmlands and toward Zachariah's farm. I was excited to see Penny and their daughter Katherine. Although it hadn't been too long, it felt like years had passed since I had seen anyone other than Malcolm, not that there was anything wrong with Malcolm. It was just strange not to see anyone else in person after long periods of time.

Glancing out at the fields, I wondered why it always seemed like they were in bloom and they never had what we would consider winter months with very few flowers growing. It probably had to do with the way Wonderland worked. Perhaps the fields rotated crops or flowers as time went on to have the land always be producing something, which would explain why there never seemed to be anyone plowing the fields. We talked about soil in biology class once, and it seemed that tilling ruined soil, which I found odd since most farmers did till. Then the documentary we had to watch called *Kiss the Ground* talked about tilling and how it was bad for the earth. Perhaps Wonderland already figured that out. Either way, the fields were gorgeous, and I wished I could stay there and admire them for hours.

Just short of an hour later, we made it to the farmhouse. We helped Zachariah unload the wagon, as he had helped us escape. After we finished, we followed him inside where Penny and Katherine were fixing lunch for the family. The moment Katherine saw me, she ran and hugged my legs in a child-sized death grip.

"Alice!"

"Hi, Katherine. I am glad to see that you are doing well." She had grown since the last time I'd seen her, which I didn't think was too long ago, but apparently I was mistaken. I wondered how much time had passed in my world but pushed back that thought as I didn't want to worry about another set of people.

I glanced up to find Penny almost appearing as if she had seen a ghost. "What's wrong Penny?"

"I… We…," she began, as if at a loss for words.

Zachariah answered for her. "I mentioned that we farmers would do anything for you, but to be honest, most of Wonderland didn't think you survived. After the Duchess gained power, we figured she defeated you."

Malcolm and I glanced at each other. So they had actually given up on us? I admitted, if I were them, I would have given up on hope too. The Duchess should have never been able to gain power while I was there. The only reason she had was because of Kate. Although I shouldn't have put one person's life in front of this entire world, I couldn't help it. She was my best friend.

Malcolm let out a long breath. "Well, it was close. But we are going to find a way to help everyone. Don't you worry."

I nodded. "We will bring back the old Wonderland… Or at least the Wonderland before this one. And thank you, Zachariah. We wouldn't have been able to hide without you. It was a miracle you showed up when you did."

"Hide?" Penny asked as she mixed the vegetables she was roasting in the kitchen. "What exactly happened?"

"I was heading back from the district after delivering flowers to the local shop when I saw these two running. They were running away from some guards, but we were able to hide before they came around the corner."

Penny nodded as she glanced down at their daughter, who was still holding on to my leg. It didn't occur to me that helping us would put their lives at risk as well. They might even use their daughter's life as a threat.

"I'm sorry to put you in this situation. If anything happens, I—"

"Don't worry about that," Penny said. "You are the symbol of Wonderland. We would do anything for you —you are the person who keeps us safe."

I was thankful for that, but I didn't feel I deserved it. It was clear that I didn't put Wonderland first compared to some others. I had been selfish when I went to save Kate. For all I knew, Malcolm could have had it under control. And in the end, Kate still lost her life. All this was for nothing.

I would make it right. I had to.

Malcolm coughed. "You don't happen to have more food and some water we could take on our journey, would you? We don't want to stay here too long, as I don't want to endanger you or your family, but we definitely need some food."

Penny nodded. "Yes, of course. We have plenty as we just harvested vegetables and fruit for the autumn months."

If we survived this, I was definitely going to beg the king and queen to give these people whatever they wanted. They deserved it after all the trouble we had caused.

"Zachariah, can you go get a pack for them while I finish up cooking? Then I can put some of the food in some containers to take."

Zachariah nodded as he went off into the back room.

Penny turned to her child, who was still wrapped around my legs. "Katherine, come help me finish cooking."

She frowned but unhooked from me and went to her mom. I glanced at Malcolm with a half smile.

"I wouldn't want to let go either."

My eyes widened, and I could feel my cheeks turn red.

He laughed as he gestured to the table. "Let's take a look at this map and see if we can find what we are looking for."

I nodded and we headed over to the table. He rolled it out. It had everything clearly marked. I glanced around to find that the Flower District was now north of the capital. So that did change.

"How accurate do you think the map is?" I asked. "I mean, it had been a setup to find us."

Malcolm shrugged. "The funny thing about maps in Wonderland is that they are never inaccurate. They change the moment the world changes. They are interactive too, see?" He pressed his finger on the Flower District, and it enlarged and the streets were visible now.

I gasped. "That is so cool! I mean, my phone can do that in my world, but a cool-looking map like that doing it is so much more awesome!"

"I doubt they would make up a fake one of these, as it would take a lot of work. They probably figured they would just catch us and wouldn't have to worry about it."

That made sense. And they probably assumed they had enough people to capture us. Clearly they were mistaken, as it would take an army and then some to stop Malcolm. "So then where do we need to go?"

Malcolm glanced at Penny, who was in the kitchen making us some food. I felt a bit guilty, but she didn't seem to mind providing us with a meal. I understood Malcolm was suspicious as he didn't know them like I did. But they had saved my life and helped us more than once. I knew they wouldn't do anything to jeopardize our mission.

"They won't tell on us."

"I don't think they willingly would go and say anything, but if they are found out, I don't want to risk them telling the soldiers. The less they know, the safer they will be."

That made sense. One didn't tell a secret unless they needed to in case someone forced it out of them. There was always that possibility.

Malcolm whispered, "The Dodo is over in this area. It will be a two-day trek, but I think it will be simple enough. We won't have to go through any districts—or at least where the people are—and we don't have to go through the Dark Forest."

"That's good." I let out a breath. Although I had been spending more time in the Dark Forest, if I could go around it, I would. I would be a happy girl if I never had to set foot in that dreary place, even if it was nice to have alone time with Malcolm. I'd much rather be alone with him somewhere else.

Malcolm rolled up the map as Zachariah came out of the back with a pack to put the food in. I watched as Penny filled the containers with food and added two canisters of water.

Katherine frowned. "Do you really have to go?"

I knelt down. "Yes, but I will be back. I promise."

Zachariah handed the supplies to Malcolm. "You two be careful. And if you need anything, just let us know."

I nodded. "Thank you. For everything. We will be back after we have fixed this and will repay our debt."

"Saving Wonderland will be enough to pay us back. Just stay safe," Penny said as she picked up Katherine.

I nodded. "We will."

Two days of hiking. Great.

I was tired—I hadn't had a good night's sleep in days. All I wanted right now was a nice bed to sleep in and the feeling of safety. But that wouldn't happen until the Duchess was gone and Wonderland was safe. And Kate was back to our world.

It was quiet, just like it had been when we first stepped out of the Dark Forest to survey what had happened. That was lucky for us, as we didn't want to run into anyone who might report which way we were heading. Zachariah had mentioned that most of the farmers were on our side, but that could have been an exaggeration. We also didn't have any way to tell who was a farmer and who was a guard or townsfolk from a distance, so it was better to assume everyone was an enemy at that point.

All of that reminded me of when I first arrived to Wonderland and how people had a dark cloud over their features. They all wanted to turn me in since my face was clear. The only difference was we had more people then to help take down the circus, and I could easily tell who had been affected. But this time it was friends who we would eventually have to fight, and I knew facing my fears would be easier than facing them.

We made it to the edge of the forest, and my shoulders relaxed a little. At least now we wouldn't be spotted easily out in the open. We could also hide if we heard someone coming or lose anyone chasing us. That all made me feel a bit more secure.

As we ventured farther, I realized that the forest we were in was quite familiar. The trees were large and tall. Could this be the forest we went through when I first came here?

"You mentioned that we wouldn't have to go through any of the district centers. So where exactly is the Dodo's hideout? You sort of generally pointed at the map back there in case Zachariah and Penny were listening in."

Malcolm stopped and pulled out the map. "When I said that we didn't have to go through any district centers, that wasn't completely true. We just won't be going through any active districts. We will be going through the White and Red Kingdom. I think we will be able to get there by nightfall, and we can spend the night in a nice bed. Hopefully they aren't too dusty."

That was why this forest seemed familiar—we were heading to the Red and White Kingdom just like we had when I first came to Wonderland. We hadn't been back to the Red and White Kingdom since the circus was destroyed. I presumed it was because there were too many bad memories there, as it was where Howard was killed. Since no one else brought it up, I never brought it up either. Now here we were, journeying through it.

"Do you think they will have anyone there in case we do show up? I mean, that and the Heart Kingdom seem like good places to keep some guards."

Malcolm shrugged. "No way to know, really. If I

were the Duchess and paranoid someone was going to come after me, I would have all my strongest men surrounding me. There are a lot of places to hide in Wonderland, and sending any of them out could be a waste of time. It made sense the guards in each town were given instructions on being on the lookout for us, but to send any others out to isolated areas wouldn't be that wise."

That made perfect sense to me. It was why I liked staying with Malcolm instead of him going out on his own without me.

Malcolm put away the map. "But we better keep on going—rather get there before night comes. Then I can survey around to make sure my hunch is right."

I nodded. "Right. Let's go."

We ventured through the forest, my legs tired and my body wanting to stop. After all the running and adrenaline, I really wanted to take a nap. I pressed on, however, as this place was a lot easier to trek compared to the Dark Forest. I wished we could have stayed out there all that time, but I knew it was less safe, which was strange to think as so many creatures lived in the Dark Forest that wanted to eat me.

Birds flew overhead, cawing and calling out to one

another. It was peculiar that some animals in Wonderland were the same as my world, and then there are beings like those in the Dark Forest, not to mention Melvin and Chase, who were humans with animal ears and powers associated with that. Chase could teleport wherever he wanted, and Malcolm was able to use illusions.

"Hey, a thought just occurred to me. You and Chase have powers, but do Melvin and Davis have any powers I should be aware of?"

Malcolm wrinkled his nose. "They did at one time, but they too have curses on them to keep them from using them. Davis could make anyone fall asleep with a word, and Melvin could get anyone to tell the truth. Just like me, they used them a little more than they should have. The only person who still can use their powers is Chase, and that is only because he is convenient for traveling to your world. Otherwise, he probably would have been given the same curse."

I nodded. That made sense. "Except he is cursed, in a way."

Malcolm shrugged. "Supposedly, but honestly I wonder if that was a lie too. He never seemed to mind following the Duchess's orders before. Hard to think she is forcing his hand in all this."

I wanted to argue the opposite, as Chase seemed to be really struggling at the end, but I decided not to. Either way, he was our enemy currently, and only he could change that fact.

The sun was beginning to set, and we arrived at the Red and White Kingdom. The grand chess pieces welcomed us as we ventured down what I believed were once lively streets. It appeared the same as it did when I was first brought here, minus a few pillars that got damaged in the last fight.

"Why didn't this place change?" I asked as we made our way through the streets, searching for any signs of others.

Malcolm shrugged. "Each time Wonderland changes, the capitals aren't affected and just sort of rot, so to speak. Alice wanted us to remember this place, so she made a law that the Red and White Kingdom and the Heart Kingdom would stay so we would remember what happened and not repeat it."

That made a little sense. "Except Wonderland is repeating itself now, isn't it?"

"Sort of. More like, someone corrupt just wants all the power." He laughed. "So yeah, I guess it is."

"But I suppose we will change that."

He nodded. "Yeah, we will."

There didn't appear to be anyone lurking around, which made sense from what Malcolm said. Once we circled back around, we went into the palace where their hangout used to be. We surveyed the rooms and found that all the weapons were still there and ready to use, along with a few places to sleep for the night that weren't completely covered in dust. Taking out some of the food that Penny had packed, I handed a bit to Malcolm.

"Thank you."

We ate in silence as we glanced around the den that brought back memories of Howard explaining to me who Alice was. It was crazy to think of how much time had gone by.

"What were the other kingdoms like? I mean, I've seen them in their state now, but what were they like when they were in power?"

Malcolm took another bite of his bread, then let out a sigh. "Horrible. I mean, the Heart Kingdom was always truly horrible, as the Heart Queen was a sadistic psychopath, but the Red and White Kingdom… It started out fair, and I had hope. But then after Alice left but things slowly spiraled out of control as the two halves of the kingdom started fighting. Of course then all the citizens got caught in the middle and chaos ensued."

So what the stories had said about those kingdoms were true. "It sounds like it."

"Then Alice came back and saved us yet again. Then she left for good." Malcolm stopped, as if reminiscing about Alice. I felt a bit jealous that he still thought of her, even after all these years.

I wanted to change the subject, even though I knew there was no possible way she mattered to him like that anymore. That was a long time ago, and I was here. "But the Dream Kingdom is fine, right? I mean, they have lasted this long and they don't seem corrupt."

"You are right. The Dream Kingdom is perfect. It has never faltered—never has anything been placed above the importance of its citizens. It truly is the perfect kingdom."

My heart felt as if it were going to break. "And because of me it is in ruin."

Malcolm shook his head. "No, the Duchess knew that the Dream Kingdom wouldn't fall and she planned all this decades ago. She and Chase."

Another reason my heart felt as if it were going to break. Chase had been in on this the entire time. I couldn't believe he didn't say anything and didn't try to help. What was he thinking?

"How long do you think they planned it?"

"Since the fall of the Red and White Kingdom. That was when the Duchess kicked Chase out and he seemed to be on his own. But we all knew better. We knew he was a loyal cat. But Howard believed in him, and so the group gave him a chance."

"Do you think Howard knew and was hoping Chase would come forward about it?"

He shrugged. "Who knows? It was because of Chase that Howard was killed, in more ways than one."

I decided not to push the subject. He was right though. Chase was trying to get me captured that night. If he hadn't done that, Howard wouldn't have died.

The question was, would he help us in the very end? Or would his loyalty always be to the Duchess?

Chapter Twelve

Morning came and I woke to find myself leaning against Malcolm. We'd ended up falling asleep on the couch in the den instead of retiring to the rooms. I liked this better as I felt more alert sleeping on a couch than in a bed. In a bed, I felt like anyone could sneak in to this palace and get the advantage over us, but staying in the den made me feel I would notice anything wrong. Whether that was true or not, I didn't have to find out the hard way.

Realizing I was leaning against Malcolm still, I quickly got up, rather flustered even though we had been sharing the same room in the Dark Forest, mainly due to my fear of the spider returning. This was more intimate, however, as I could still feel his warm chest. If I could, I would have snuggled like that for hours. But we had a job to finish.

My movement woke him. He rubbed his eyes and smiled at me.

"Morning already?"

I nodded as I moved away from him some more. "Yeah. Seems to be."

"Well, we better head out as soon as we can. Then we should make it to the Dodo's by sundown. Speaking of which, we should grab some more weapons since they still appear to be in good condition."

"Yeah, what's another sword to carry?" I sarcastically replied as my hip ached at the thought. It was bad enough to have one sword weighing me down, but the thought of two made me want to cringe. But having the extra weapons would be smarter, so I helped gather our packs, and we headed to the armory.

"It surprises me all these weapons are still here. I presumed the cat would have come back and taken them all."

"Perhaps he wanted us to come here and get them."

Malcolm let out a breath. "Although I love how pure you are and how you try to see the good in people, I can't help but be a little jealous that you always are on his side."

I put my hands on my hips. "It's not that I am always on his side. I just… I don't know. He was a good friend, and I don't like the idea of turning my back on him when I could possibly help him. We don't know his whole story."

Malcolm's eyes turned dark. "I know his whole story. I know all the times he snuck into the Heart Castle and tried to bring me down. I know the many times he almost killed Davis and Melvin. I knew when he made it look like an accident but took out people who had been important to us because they said something rude to the Duchess or just didn't bow once. I have seen him do all these things. Were they just because of the Duchess? Well… He never seemed to not have a smile on his face when he hurt those people."

I frowned, realizing that he had known Chase much longer, and what I had seen was just a glimpse of all the destruction he had caused. I opened my mouth to say something but then closed it as there was nothing for me to say.

Malcolm pinched the bridge of his nose. "I'm sorry, Alice, it's just been a long couple of weeks. It doesn't help that I don't like the way he looks at you. He… It doesn't matter. It was a long time ago, and I need to move on. The two of us are here, right now, and we need to focus on stopping the Duchess. And if it is possible, maybe saving Chase. Maybe. I'm not going out of my way though."

I smiled. "Thank you."

"Now pick your weapons. I would advise getting another sword and at least one knife."

I nodded and peered through all the weapons. I picked up a dagger and another katana that was lying round. Luckily there were fasteners I could slip the sword and sheath in to sling it around my body. That way both my hands were free and all I had to worry about was weight.

But luckily I had been working on my strength training since coming to Wonderland. It wouldn't be too hard to carry these as long as we didn't have to go up any large mountains or hills.

The moment I thought that, I knew it was going to

happen—the Dodo was probably going to live on some large mountainside that we would have to scale. I sighed and debated asking Malcolm but knew I'd rather just find out once we got there than think about it all day.

After gathering all that we needed, we ventured back into the wilderness. By the end of the day, we would have our answers on how to save Wonderland.

I couldn't wait.

Would it be too immature to say "Are we there yet?"

I felt like saying it to just pass the time, as I was tired and getting a bit cranky from walking so far. Although we trained a lot in the Dark Forest, having to walk all day toward a destination you just wanted to be at already was nerve-racking. I just wanted this to be over with. I was tired, hungry, and was done with having to worry whether or not anyone was following us.

Honestly, I just wanted to go home.

But what was home for me? Every time I thought about having to go back to normal, I thought back to Davis and Melvin and how we would all get together to explore or just have a meal. I missed the lunches at school we used to have together and all the memories, whether they were all good or not. I thought of them the most—did that mean I had accepted Wonderland as my home?

I still cared about everyone in my world, even my two sisters whom I didn't get along with. But here I felt accepted and as if I could do anything. Here I was—I hate to say it—important. At home I was average and always fighting for what I wanted to do. Here, well, I was fighting, but not in the same way. Here I fought for Wonderland, but I could be myself.

Playing with the thought, I wondered if I could set up an art shop here. I could teach people how to paint, sell some of my paintings, and be doing what I wanted to do in my world. Here, though, it seemed achievable, whereas in my world it didn't seem as likely as many things could destroy a business in a blink of an eye, not to mention art school would cost a lot. Here I could find an artist and mentor under them for a while, and travel.

This world had everything I ever wanted—adventures, beauty, a society not centralized by money but by making sure everyone was fed and cared for. As long as there wasn't anyone taking over Wonderland, of course. But even so, I felt like I was betraying everyone I cared for in my world. At the same time, they wouldn't remember me, so they wouldn't have to worry.

I let out a sigh. Malcolm glanced over. "Don't worry, we will reach there by nightfall."

I laughed. "Not that. Well, kind of. I am tired. But I was just thinking about Wonderland and what will happen when we win."

"Ah."

He didn't add anything more than that, as the discussion of what I would do after Wonderland was restored was still a problematic one. He had a point. I didn't know what it was like to live forever, or nearly forever. Would this feeling of regret only get worse as time went on? Or would I move past it? There was no way of knowing, but I felt that I would have even more regret if I went back to my world. Either way, it would be unknown and I would have to choose.

I interlaced my fingers with Malcolm. "But I need to focus on the now. We will reach Dodo, and he will come up with a plan, and we will save Wonderland."

"Exactly. Focus is key."

We pushed farther into the woods. As we moved closer to the edge of Wonderland, I noticed it was becoming darker and there were fewer animals moving around. It wasn't dark like the sun was setting or darkness like that of the Dark Forest, but more as if it were losing saturation. The colors were becoming bleak as if life didn't make it out all the way out here. It was as if the magic of Wonderland was fading.

"How much land is there outside of Wonderland?"

Malcolm shrugged. "Not quite sure, to be honest. No one has gone too far outside. Or, at least, none that have returned."

Well, that wasn't reassuring. "But Dodo isn't too far from the edge."

"No, he's right on it. He knows better than to go too far. He's still within some of the energy, or magic, of Wonderland. The shift just isn't strong enough to affect out here. But any farther… well… it is said that we with roles will die as Wonderland is what gives us life."

"That's… different." I had no idea what else to say to that.

He chuckled. "That's one way to put it. I always wonder how far out the others made it before something happened or if it is even true. It's not necessarily something I ever wanted to find out."

I squeezed his hand tighter. It never occurred to me that Wonderland could seem small after such a long life. And not to mention not knowing what was on the other side of the land.

CHAPTER THIRTEEN

"You have got to be kidding me." I stared up at the steep mountain that we had to climb.

Malcolm raised an eyebrow. "Did you not notice that the map said this part of Wonderland was mountainous? It makes it harder for people to wander outside the boundaries of magic."

I sighed. "No. I did not. I should have figured. Nothing is ever easy, is it?"

He laughed. "Nope. Are you ready?"

No. "I guess."

We started to climb. Luckily it wasn't so steep that if I slipped, I would fall to my death, but it was steep enough that I had to crawl up so I didn't slip and fall. If I wasn't careful, I could end up rolling down the mountain like in *The Princess Bride*. That did not look fun. I would probably get a concussion, or worse, from one of the rocks.

Ignore the rocks. Ignore the rocks.

There were many things that could be more difficult to venture through, or at least that was what I kept telling myself. It could be a swamp or lava or a steeper cliff. All those would have been much worse. I took a deep breath. Yes, much worse than this. I glanced back down. Even though it was a steep slope and not straight down, my fear of heights struck me hard. I clenched the grass I was holding on to.

Malcolm glanced my way. "It will be fine. You will only slide—you won't fall."

"I know, but I really don't like it. Heights suck."

"Would you rather go down in a cave and be underground with the fear the ceiling will cave in?"

I pondered that thought. "No, that option also sucks. All options suck. Nothing is easy in Wonderland."

"I find this stuff easier than trying to navigate in your world though."

"That's fair. My world makes everything more complicated, not to mention how large it is and how many people there are. At least here things are sort of finite, even if there is a Dark Forest where everything wants to kill you. My world actually has plenty of those, truth be told."

"Oh really? I wish I'd gotten to visit them."

I rolled my eyes. "You are so strange."

Malcolm chuckled. "I suppose I am. But isn't everyone a little bit odd. At least anyone worth talking to."

He had a point there.

An hour passed as we ventured up the slope. After a while, we decided to stop and take a break. My arms and legs were sore. After all that conditioning, that was still quite the workout. I turned and found that I could see almost all of Wonderland from up here. I could see the Red and White Kingdom from which we came, the fields of the Flower District, the Duchess's mansion.

It was beautiful.

"Taking in the sights?" Malcolm asked as he opened the canister of water and took a drink.

I nodded. "It's so beautiful. I mean, I have been to all these places, but looking from above just makes it so…"

"Wonderful?" Malcolm smirked as he handed me the water. I took a sip.

"Yeah. I wish I could paint it someday."

"Perhaps you will."

I wasn't sure if he meant in general or that he had accepted that I probably wouldn't be leaving Wonderland anytime soon. At that rate, I didn't expect to go back home. I just hoped that when Wonderland was taken over, that my existence in the real world had disappeared. I didn't want my parents worrying as I wasn't in my bed at home. They were probably already awake and checking up on me. I couldn't imagine their worry to find me gone. Then there was Kate's mother…

"How much farther do we need to go?" I asked, shoving such thoughts behind me. I couldn't waste energy worrying about them but had to push forward to make it right.

Malcolm shook his head. "Not too much farther. Probably another fifteen minutes. Just needed a break for some water."

Fifteen minutes was probably all we had before it

would be pitch-black. We turned back upward to start our ascent once again. I noticed Malcolm began to climb a bit faster, and I did as well. My thighs, hamstrings, and biceps burned and ached, but I didn't give up, mainly because I knew if I stopped, then it would take all my effort to get back going again.

We reached the top, or at least a flattened area, and I collapsed on the ground. Malcolm gave me a moment, then extended his hand.

"We are almost there. Hurry before it is dark or I can't find the exact spot."

I nodded and grabbed his arm. I grimaced as I stood up and followed him. At least this part was flat, I told myself, and that we were almost there.

Malcolm searched around on all the walls. I wasn't sure what he was looking for—if it was some kind of marking or what. By the looks of it though, there weren't any houses up there. Where could Dodo be?

Finally Malcolm stopped and knocked on a rock.

"Uh… what are you doing?" I asked.

"You can't tell, but it's a door."

I shrugged. "I guess this is Wonderland. It's not the strangest thing I have seen."

Malcolm chuckled. "That's for sure."

Suddenly the piece of rock swung open, and I jumped back, startled. I felt my foot hit the edge of the flat area, and I almost fell back. Luckily, Malcolm grabbed me.

A man with shaggy white hair and beard stared at both of us. He had rough skin that clung to his bones and eyes that seemed like they had seen things I didn't even want to imagine. It was no wonder he was out there like a hermit. He literally appeared like one.

"No." The man slammed the door shut again. I just stared at it. Did he really deny us before we could even talk? Had all this been for nothing?

CHAPTER FOURTEEN

Malcolm sighed. "He's always like this."

"How's a crazed man like that going to help us?" I asked as my heart began to race. We needed him to save Wonderland—we needed him to save Kate. He wasn't what I imagined—he was more like Radagast in *The Hobbit* but not kind and didn't seem to want to help. No, I didn't imagine he could do anything.

Malcolm wrapped his arm around me. "It will be okay. I will get him to talk to us."

I slowly nodded as Malcolm knocked. The door opened again, and this time Malcolm stuck his boot in the way of it closing.

"I said I wasn't helping," the old main exclaimed. "Why would I ever want to help you? You tried to kill me! More than once!"

"You will listen to us, and you will help." Malcolm's voice was stern.

Dodo's eyes narrowed. "And what if I say no?"

"Then I have nothing to lose and I will use my powers on you with my dying breath. Then you won't cause anyone problems ever again."

The two of them held each other's glare, then the door fully opened. "Fine, I will listen. But I'm not promising anything."

"As usual."

Dodo shot Malcolm a look as we entered his cave-house thing. It was actually a lot nicer on the inside than I thought it would be. I glanced around to find paintings that were almost like the Pre-Raphaelite era. They had to be oil based and had taken quite some time. And there were so many of them.

"Where did you get these paintings?" I asked, even though it really didn't matter at the moment. The artist in me had to ask, for later.

"Oh those." The Dodo appeared smug. "I painted those. Now that I am retired and don't have to deal with the drama that surrounds Wonderland, I have become quite inspired. The original Alice brought me oils once when she visited, and I was able to replicate them with pigments in this world. She is the reason I paint and wasn't killed." He shot Malcolm another look, but Malcolm ignored it.

My jaw dropped. He painted those? There was no way. They almost appeared as works of Waterhouse, who was one of my favorite artists.

Dodo went on. "Speaking of which, Malcolm, you know better than to drag me into such troubles, and yet here you are—threatening me."

"A lot is at stake now. You are the wisest man in all of Wonderland, not to mention you are one of few who haven't been affected."

Dodo frowned. "So everyone is really brainwashed by the Duchess?"

"Everyone. Even Bill and Melvin and the others. The citizens are so-so, but I am not sure who to trust, and there isn't all that much they can do. As for those who have roles, I assume you and any of the others outside of Wonderland survived the change, per usual."

"Per usual." Dodo ran his hands through his beard. "But you took a big bet to assume that."

"That I did. But I can tell you aren't affected since you slammed the door in our faces. If you had let us in right away, I would have been suspicious."

Dodo let out a laugh. "You are one smart lad. No, I don't assume the others were affected either. Even though we all live on the edge, I haven't seen any of them in quite some time. They are more reclusive than I am."

"Which is why I came to you rather than them. I doubt any would help, nor do I think they can come up with anything that I couldn't. You are the only one."

Dodo stopped stroking his beard. "How did you manage it? How did you get away?"

Malcolm hesitated. "Yes. Luckily Alice and I were able to get to the Dark Forest in time."

He laughed. "You and the Dark Forest. I don't know how you ever survived. I guess you are just part of that place now."

Malcolm didn't say anything as his eyes darkened. I decided to change the subject. "But you do know a way I can get my power back and we can defeat the

Duchess?"

He pursed his lips, then nodded to the kitchen. "How about I whip up something to eat? I assume the two of you are starving."

My stomach growled as if it had heard. Dodo laughed.

"Well, I guess that is a yes. I will get some food going then. Does stew sound all right?"

"That would be great," I said and turned to Malcolm, who also nodded.

"Take a seat. I will be right back. Malcolm, would you like some tea?"

"Of course," Malcolm said as we both took a seat. As Dodo fixed us up some food, I glanced at the paintings again.

"These are really magnificent, you know. I can't believe he painted them. And apparently makes his own paint too."

"Well, he is old. He had a lot of time to get this good."

My eyes scanned all the walls. It was strange that they could appear so much like *Ophelia, Lilith, The Lady of Shallot*, but have a certain Wonderland essence to them. Perhaps he was connected to my world by art, as the dreams were.

"I wonder if I lived forever if I could become this good."

Malcolm peered at me through the corner of his eyes. "You mean if you stayed?"

I shrugged. "It's a possibility. We don't know if it is possible for me to go back."

Malcolm didn't say anything, so I kept staring at the paintings, wondering how long it took him to paint them all.

After fifteen minutes or so, Dodo reappeared with bowls of soup. He placed them on his small dining table, and we got up and moved over to join him. He brought out a teapot as well and poured Malcolm a cup of tea.

"Alice, would you like one?"

I nodded. "Sure."

The sweet smell of bergamot came wafting off the tea, and I instantly knew it was Earl Grey. I glanced over to Malcolm, who was hiding his glee. It was one of his favorite flavors, if there was, in fact, any flavor he didn't like.

I took a spoonful of the stew and blew on it. I tried to push back the curiosity of where he would get supplies for food. It was Wonderland, and I probably didn't want to know. I would eat anything at this rate.

I took a bite and was immediately in love. The beef, or whatever red meat it was, melted in my mouth like my mother's pot roast. The food made me miss my parents, but I couldn't help but smile as it was so delicious. I took another spoonful and savored the thyme and oregano-like flavors.

"I see Alice likes my cooking. I am glad."

Malcolm stirred his tea. "And yet you were going to throw us out. Typical Dodo."

"It was more that I wanted to throw you out, Hatter. I have no quarrels with Alice. She is Alice."

I took a sip of the tea. It was quite delicious as well, but I had a feeling Malcolm would be the real judge of that. I watched as he took a sip and grinned a little. He approved.

"I am not *the* Alice though, just Alice." I ate some of the food. "If it weren't for me, none of this would be happening."

Dodo laughed. "That isn't true. That is why you were called to Wonderland. Wonderland needs you. I'm sure Howard told you the same."

I nodded. "That he did. A while back."

"How is dear Howard? I do miss my pupil."

My gaze darted to Malcolm, as I had no idea how I would tell him the bad news. Malcolm set his teacup down. "He died when we took down the circus. He was cut down right in front of me."

Dodo frowned. "I see. Well then, he finally got to wake up as a butterfly. I bet he is the most beautiful butterfly in all of existence." He took a deep breath. "Well then, let us finish eating and we can discuss you, Alice."

We ate the rest of our food in silence. I felt bad that Howard was brought up and we had to mention his death. I was surprised Malcolm didn't go into detail and blame Chase. Perhaps it didn't matter in the end.

After our stomachs were satisfied, Dodo had us retire to the couches.

"So to answer your question, I do know what to do to help you Alice, but you are not going to like it."

"I will do anything," I said. "And I mean that."

Dodo glanced to Malcolm, then turned back to me. "You will have to give up your life to Wonderland. And I don't mean die—I mean you will have to serve Wonderland for the rest of eternity. This world will then be cut off from yours, for traveling at least. The dreams will still be connected, and there will never be a new Alice. You will always be *the* Alice who saves Wonderland. Forever."

Although I knew that was a possibility and that I could be stuck here anyway, I was taken aback by how he worded it. I would have that position forever. I leaned back on the couch and took a deep breath.

Forever was a long time to hear out loud.

CHAPTER FIFTEEN

"No," Malcolm stated. "I won't let her stay here."

Dodo shrugged. "It's the only way to bring back her power. She has to sacrifice herself."

"She can't. She doesn't deserve having to live an eternity here. You know as well as I that these lives are not a blessing—that forever is a long time to bear."

"Well, you don't have much choice. The options are clearly only getting captured by the Duchess and being executed or an eternity serving this land. This option doesn't seem that bad to me."

"It's my choice, Malcolm, or have we not gone over this enough times?" I shot him a look.

He shook his head. "I have seen this world rise and crumble so many times. While it is a blessing, Alice, to have you in my life—and I want nothing more than to keep you close for the rest of my life—I also don't want you to have to suffer that responsibility."

"You keep contradicting yourself, Malcolm. You want me here or you don't?"

"I don't want you to make the same mistake I did, all right?"

I furrowed my brow. "What do you mean?"

Malcolm was silent, then turned away. Dodo coughed.

"What he means is, anyone who has a role wasn't originally from this world. They are actually humans from your world."

My eyes widened as I turned to Malcolm. "Is this true?"

He hesitated. "Something like that."

"Why did you never tell me that?"

He shrugged. "Never came up."

"That's a lie. You could have mentioned it many

times when we talked about whether I should choose Wonderland or not. You could have said you grew up in my world, and then I would have understood why you have been so determined for me to stay in my world."

"It was a long time ago. Your world wasn't the same as mine. I chose Wonderland because I grew up as a peasant in medieval England. There were plagues and war that went on for generations. You have no idea what life was life for me back then."

"Wouldn't understand? You think my era is better? There are so many people in the world that resources are diminishing. We are destroying our world and think there are no consequences to that. People have no empathy, there is always war, and we have lost connection to nature. So while living forever and turning my back on those in my world does seem hard, living in a world full of adventure and the people I care about seems like a good choice to me."

Malcolm took in my words for a moment. "That was what I had thought too. Then the Queen of Hearts showed up. Then this world became violent, and it really isn't much different. You only have been here a couple of years, and you can see the dangers it possesses. Even if we take out the Duchess, another one like her will come around. They might defeat you and then what? We will be lost without an Alice, and our world will turn out to be just like yours. Are you ready to have to keep battling to make sure that doesn't happen?"

I frowned. He had a point. I couldn't mess up or else Wonderland would be without an Alice, and who knew what would happen then.

"I'm willing to live my life for Wonderland. It is my fault it is the way it is now. I can't just turn my back on it."

Dodo clapped his hands together. "Well, if that is settled, is there anything else you need, or will you two be on your merry way?"

Did he really hate guests that much? I felt like I was missing something, as the argument with Malcolm had distracted me. Then it hit me.

"What about Kate?" I asked.

He shook his head. "Who?"

"My friend Kate. She was from my world and was forcibly brought here. She disappeared before I could save her... Is there a way to bring her back and return her to my world?"

Dodo stroked his beard. "There might be a way, yes, but what I'm not sure. This hasn't happened before."

"Please, there has to be a way."

"I suppose there is a possibility. Once you return your powers, you might be able to wish her back into existence. I can't promise anything. But if you send her back, which you would have to or she will disappear again, she will forget you and everything. You, of course, will remember everything. That will be the price you pay to be in this world. Memories that will never fade away, no matter how much time has passed."

I nodded. "That is worth it. I don't think I would be able to return to my world, knowing the truth anyway."

"Well then, I guess it is settled. You must defeat the Duchess, return your power, and you can bring your friend back. Then you will stay in Wonderland forever."

I kept nodding. So it was decided. I really would be staying there. I glanced over at Malcolm, who was frowning with his arms crossed. He still didn't like the idea of me staying. Although I knew it was because he didn't want me to suffer what it was like to be eternal, I couldn't help but feel a sting in my heart. Did he really not relish the idea that I would be there with him?

A lot could happen in an eternity, however. What if the two of us broke up again? It wasn't like I could just ignore him as we would be stuck in the same land. It was large, but not that large. I wondered if Wonderland was really the same size as Salem and the surrounding small towns like Keizer and West Salem. If that was the case, I would run into him all the time, just like in Salem. Sometimes it was the worst.

"So will you two be on your way now?" Dodo asked.

Malcolm eyed him. "I was hoping we could stay here for the night. It's not like we can descend this mountain in the dark."

"Right. I forget about light and dark. Sometimes I don't sleep for days, believe it or not."

I definitely could believe that.

"But I suppose if you walked all the way here from Red and White Kingdom, then you would be quite tired."

The edge of Malcolm's mouth flinched. "Right. We are very tired. But first I wanted to come up with some plans to take down the Duchess. I presume you have some ideas. You were the mastermind that Howard always looked up to, after all."

Dodo hesitated, and I could see sweat on his brow. Was he really this uncomfortable with guests? I felt a little bad putting him off like that, but it was the only option we had.

"Right," he said. "For Howard. We can discuss some plans. I presume the Duchess has her same manor?"

Malcolm nodded. "That she does."

"Well, I should have some maps of her estate. I will be right back."

Dodo left us to go in the back room. I wondered how far his home extended into the rock. I glanced to Malcolm, who was staring down the hallway.

"What's wrong?"

He turned to me and smiled. "Nothing. Don't worry about it. Just make sure to have your katana within reach at all times."

I nodded slowly as we waited for Dodo to reappear.

Dodo reappeared with a few pieces of paper. His sweat covered his entire face now. Did he really hate people that much? I supposed if I had been away from people for generations, I would feel awkward or sweat too.

"Here are some old maps. As long as she didn't renovate, I think it all should be accurate."

Malcolm took the papers and put them on the coffee table. "It appears accurate to me, at least for when we were there last. Let's see…" Malcolm bit his thumbnail.

"She is probably somewhere surrounded by guards but also where she can look out on her precious land she just had to have."

I glanced at the map, trying to remember all the rooms. "Do you think she will mostly be in the same one she was in when she was waiting for me with Kate? It was large, you could have guards in there easily, and it had a balcony one could look down on people with. I mean, that's what she does, right?"

Malcolm nodded. "You have a point. That settles where she probably is ordering people around. Now the question is, where would she put the orb of Wonderland?"

"Ah," Dodo commented. "That is how she took over Wonderland."

I nodded. "I gave her the orb in return for letting my friend go, but it was too late and she disappeared. Apparently the countdown wasn't exact, and Chase didn't take into consideration the time it took to grab her and then stop the execution."

"So he is still a loyal cat after all this time. That surprises me. He always seemed to hate her guts."

Malcolm interjected. "Yeah, well, a cat is a cat. You never know when they are going to betray your trust."

Dodo let out a laugh, and I ignored the both of them. "So where would she keep the orb?"

Malcolm let out a sigh. "That's the problem, isn't it? She could have hidden it somewhere, or she might have it with her."

"With her as she is surrounded by all our friends."

"Precisely."

I pondered on that. If I were paranoid and wanting to be surrounded by guards in case Malcolm came to kill me, I would keep the most powerful thing as near as possible, since that was what he was after. I wasn't sure what else she could do with it once she'd cast her spell, but if I had it in my hands, then Wonderland would go back to the way it was and she would be no more.

"She probably has it close to her. She is paranoid and wants to keep an eye on things. I am sure she has it. Maybe on a staff or something."

"That makes sense." Malcolm let out a breath. "But that makes it all the more complicated."

"How so?"

"Because now we are going to have to get in past her normal guards, defeat all our friends and Chase, and take it out of her cold, dead hands. With just the two of us."

I bit my lip. "We could just run straight at her and hope for the best."

"That is a possibility. What says you, Dodo? You are awfully quiet."

"Oh, I am just thinking. Perhaps you need not focus on the orb until the end. Perhaps focus on killing her so that the curse is broken. Then the orb will be free and you can do what you want with it to restore Wonderland."

"But how do we kill her if she is surrounded by Bill, Kenny, Davis, Melvin, and Chase?" Malcolm narrowed his eyes at Dodo. "That is, if you are still as remarkable as Howard made you out to be."

"I guess, if I had to kill the Duchess, I would look for her weakness. If she doesn't have one, then look for a weakness in someone close to her."

"You mean like Chase?" I asked.

He shrugged. "Perhaps. The Duchess has been waiting a long time, and it is apparent she has been thinking long and hard. She probably doesn't have any weak spots one can find easily. But that can't be said for the people around her. Chase has had his ups and downs, I will give him that, but he is one who will falter if Alice is involved, am I wrong?"

I slowly shook my head.

"So your best bet is getting him to repent. However, I'm not sure how far he can."

"What do you mean?" Malcolm asked.

Dodo let out a slow breath. "Howard and I knew the Duchess well. We knew her well enough to know what kind of… magic, so to speak, she was willing to use to get her way. The price is strong when one wants a lot of magic, so she typically doesn't use it. But back before these restraints were bestowed on us by Howard, she used a spell on Chase. It is like a collar, and if she pulls on it, it will hurt him, perhaps even kill him."

So that's why he couldn't tell us. He really did have a curse.

"That's terrible," I said and turned to Malcolm. "See, I told you."

He gestured with his arms, as if he really didn't care. "We all have our baggage."

I rolled my eyes and turned back to Dodo. "So you think if we can get through to him, it's possible to stop her."

He nodded. "I think so."

"Then the question is, how are we going to get into the mansion and talk to Chase? We might have to go through the others to even get close."

"I wouldn't worry about us getting into the mansion." Malcolm sighed as he rolled up the maps. "We will just have to worry about escaping."

"What do you mean?"

"I mean, Dodo has already alerted them that we are here." He eyed him. "Haven't you?"

Dodo's eyes widened. "How did you…?"

"I've survived this long, haven't I?" Malcolm smiled. "But don't worry, after all this is over, we are going to have a very long talk."

Dodo sheepishly smiled. "If it is any consolation, I did hold them off this long so you could put together a plan. And now you have a way to get in easier."

Malcolm shook his head, then gestured to me. "Let's get out of here."

CHAPTER SEVENTEEN

It was pitch-black outside still. Although the stars and moon shone in the sky above us, it was not enough for me to feel confident that I wasn't going to trip and fall and roll to my death. Odds were, I would hit a rock. There were plenty of them out there. After everything, that was not how I wanted to end this.

"Uh, I don't think I can run down," I commented with a gulp.

"We won't be going down. We will stay on this flat

area and hide. They will give up eventually. Hopefully."

That made the most sense, other than the hiding part. I peered back and found guards appearing in front of Dodo's door. Dodo pointed at where we had ran off toward. He could have pointed in the opposite direction. I let out a breath. Typical traitors. I should have figured by now not to trust anyone. Except Penny and Zachariah. They seemed to be the exception, however.

I noticed one of the soldiers wasn't wearing the same type of clothing as the others, and I could make out cat ears on the top of his head. It was Chase. That was how they were able to get here so quickly, as they didn't have to scale that mountain. He apparently could teleport on the edge of Wonderland. Just our luck.

"Chase is with them," I whispered. "What are we going to do?"

I watched as one of Chase's ears twitched, but he didn't turn our way. I gulped, wondering if he did in fact hear us, or if they twitched for a different reason. I hoped it was the latter.

Malcolm squeezed my hand. "Don't worry. I have a plan. Follow me closely."

We ventured down the leveled path. I prayed that we

wouldn't have to climb higher as I didn't think my legs could take it, and because it was a lot steeper than the first inclination. Luckily Malcolm seemed to be staying on the flat part, as if searching for something.

"Are you trying to find someone else's home? Do other people live in these rocks?"

"No, at least I don't think so. I am looking for a cave we can hide in. Even if they find the cave, it will be pitch-black, and we can attack them before they see it coming."

"Ah." Great, more fighting. I was tired and just wanted to sleep. At least my stomach was full, although that had made me even more sleepy. The caffeine from the tea was helping a bit at least.

Malcolm went on, "I'm just thankful Dodo didn't slip anything into our food. He could have really messed us up."

"Perhaps he knew no matter what you would survive and didn't want to take his chances."

He chuckled. "Probably."

We ventured farther along the mountain. I could see the guards shuffling around, but it didn't seem as if they were getting any closer to us. I pondered on why Chase didn't just transport over to us when he heard me talk.

Perhaps he was having a change of heart and we would be able to get off this mountain before they captured us.

That, or he was up to something else.

Malcolm stopped. "Here is a cave. We can wait here until they are gone."

I followed him inside. From the echo of our footsteps, it sounded like a large cave. I held on to Malcolm's shirt as he led me behind one of the rocks. He had better night vision than I ever could. He didn't seem to hesitate like one would when they were walking in the dark. Once we were settled, I let out a breath.

"You think it is a good idea to wait?" I whispered.

"There isn't much more we can do. No matter how far we run now, we won't be able to get away from them, not since Chase is with them. Going up or down is impossible in this darkness. Safely, at least."

I sat down and took a deep breath. I tried to listen to see if they would search for us around here, but I heard nothing. I couldn't see anything in the cave either. I hated being in such darkness, but it was all we could do. It reminded me of Morpheus and all the tricks he had played on me. I had dreams where I was surrounded in darkness with no way out, and he was there, taunting me.

Malcolm stayed standing, and I assumed he had his hand on the hilt of his sword as he waited. I would sit there and be his backup, as my legs were throbbing now. I apparently needed to train more, which frustrated me. How could I not have trained enough?

As he stood and I sat there, I heard steps come up to the cave. I squeezed my knees, full of fear, as I listened closely.

It sounded like only one person, as each step was after the next. It wasn't a mix of steps echoing. Whoever it was, stayed silent, as if waiting to see what we would do. I stayed there, my heart now racing. This was worse than when your parents came to check on you in the middle of the night and you tried to pretend you were asleep when really you had been awake watching anime. Way worse.

"I know you two are in here. I can hear you breathing." It was Chase. By the sounds of it, he was alone. I was right.

Malcolm didn't try to hide but stepped out to where Chase was waiting. I heard him pull out his sword. "You know what, cat? I have had it with you and am ready to put you in your place."

"Look, I know you are mad, but there is no use resisting—the Duchess won."

Malcolm let out a laugh. "You think so? Does the pet cat think so? Well, I will promise with my dying breath that I will kill you, Chase. Do you realize everything you have done? Do you realize there is little chance of Alice returning to her world? For Wonderland to be free of problems? No, you just did whatever she asked."

I peered around the rock but could barely see anything other than two figures. The details of each were darkened, but I could imagine Malcolm's face as it was full of anger. And I could imagine Chase appearing frustrated with a touch of sadness.

"I had no choice! I can't disobey her! It is like having an invisible collar around my neck. I can't do anything of my own free will."

"So said Dodo. He explained your curse. Funny, it was the first time I had heard of it. Did Howard find out and that was why you killed him?"

Chase was quiet for a moment. "I didn't kill Howard."

"No, but your actions for the Duchess did! You led Bill to the site! And that is what killed him!"

"Howard was like a father to me! I would never have

let him die!"

"So if the Duchess told you to kill him, you wouldn't have?"

"I… He was helping me with the curse. We almost had a plan to end it. If he hadn't died…"

I held my hand over my mouth. All this time, Chase could have had the curse reversed. He had not only dealt with the guilt of what had happened to Howard but also watched as it destroyed his chance of being free of the Duchess.

"I don't care what you say! You are the reason he is dead!"

I heard someone move and the clashing of swords. I understood that Chase could see in the dark, since he was a cat, but could Malcolm? Standing up, I tried to get a better look but couldn't make out anything. I stayed still, as I didn't want to get in the middle of two swords I could not see.

"Malcolm! Chase! Please stop!"

"He needs to face the consequences of his actions, Alice!" Malcolm exclaimed.

"You are one to talk!" Chase replied. "You have done as many horrifying things as I have, and yet you are accepted by everyone! I tried to seek that acceptance, and you all treated me as a suspect!"

"Were we wrong? Because by the looks of it, all our hunches were right!"

There were more clashes of swords. Suddenly I heard one fall to the ground and a thud of a body. I didn't know who fell or who lost their sword.

"Say goodbye, cat."

"Malcolm, no! Please, don't kill him!"

Suddenly I felt an arm wrap around me and cold metal against my throat.

"Drop your weapon, Malcolm," Chase's voice said from behind me. He had teleported the moment Malcolm hesitated from my shouts.

"You traitor," Malcolm stated as he dropped his sword. "You disgust me."

Suddenly there were a bunch of footsteps in the cave, and I could make out figures standing at the entrance. It was the guards Chase had come with.

Chase ordered, "I found them. Take care of Malcolm. I have Alice under control."

I really wanted to draw my weapon to prove him wrong, but I couldn't bring myself to harm Chase. I held out my hands so he could grab my weapons. As he did so, I heard him whisper.

"I'm sorry."

I didn't respond but let him grab my arm and push me forward to the mouth of the cave. I tried to be optimistic, as now we were being taken to the mansion except for the one person who could possibly help take her down.

CHAPTER EIGHTEEN

We didn't have to travel across Wonderland, as Chase could transport us all the way. I missed being able to go through portals like that, but it felt completely different than it used to. When we traveled before, it was always for an adventure or mission, not to be taken to the enemy. Except once when Bill captured me.

I also wasn't sure if I felt more comforted or not that it was Chase taking me in rather than some strange soldier. It hurt that he betrayed us, but I also didn't have to wonder what the stranger was going to do or say. Not that we had long to talk as what would have taken the better half of two days now only took a few seconds. It wasn't like when Bill arrested me the first time we met.

It was also awkward because neither Chase, Malcolm, nor I wanted to talk after everything that had happened. A lot had come out just moments before. Malcolm blamed Chase for Howard's death, Chase had lost his chance of a free life when Howard died, and I'd gotten in the middle of it all and caused Chase to use me to get Malcolm to back down. It was all a lot to take in.

I knew Chase wouldn't have hurt me, and I would have thought Malcolm would have deduced the same, but he threw his sword down as if he believed him. Did Malcolm think Chase would have really hurt me? That was hard for me to believe as we had been through a lot. Then again, he had cost Kate her life, and practically brought down Wonderland.

But I would bring her back and save Wonderland. I had to.

Chase stayed close to me, but I could tell he was keeping an eye on Malcolm. I almost could see the anime electric bolt appearing between their eyes as they glared at each other. I ignored them both, as I wasn't going to get in the middle of it. Again.

We ventured through the gardens of the Duchess's mansion. I was surprised Chase didn't just appear in the middle of the mansion like he always used to do with the Dream Palace. Perhaps the Duchess's security would actually stab him, or perhaps he thought Malcolm could try to make an escape. Did he teleport all the way out here to help us? Or was I overthinking it?

I knew I was probably overthinking it, as I tended to do that quite often. As we ventured toward the mansion, a familiar face appeared.

"Well, if it isn't Malcolm."

"Hello, Bill. Did you finally find Kenny?"

Bill pointed his finger at Malcolm. "That is not funny! Do you have any idea how much trouble I was in for letting the two of you escape?"

It was strange that he was under the Duchess' spell, and yet he still had a similar personality. When he was under Morpheus' darkness, he wasn't as playful as he was right now. It was as if they stayed being the same personality, but never remembered that we were their friends.

Malcolms lips turned into a sly smile. "As much trouble you will be in once I kill the Duchess?"

Bill narrowed his eyes and drew his sword. Before he could do anything, Chase held out his arm.

"Ah, ah. No hurting the prisoners. Not yet at least."

Bill pouted, almost like Kenny used to. "Ah, but he's caused me so many problems."

"Well, if you just didn't obsess over Kenny so much, Alice wouldn't have gotten the upper hand, now would she have?"

Bill sighed. "I guess not." He put his sword away. "Besides, the Duchess has a lot more in store for them than I ever could."

I didn't like how he said that. What would the Duchess do once we set foot in front of her? This was definitely the easiest way to get to her room, but not having any weapons was not ideal. Nor was being outnumbered and the fact that she had the sphere. But we would win—or at least that was what I kept telling myself.

I glanced over to Chase again, who was purposefully looking away from both me and Malcolm. He didn't want to face what he had done to us. I wished we could talk it out—see if there was a way we could make it out of all of this and save Wonderland. If he just told us what we needed to do to reverse his curse, I was sure we could do it. But he didn't say anything. Did he really not have hope we would win? Or was he planning something else?

We made it to the mansion doors, and Chase frowned a little as he peered over to Malcolm. Maybe he did expect Malcolm to get us out of there and hoped we wouldn't let ourselves be taken in so easily. Malcolm held his gaze though, and Chase rolled his catlike eyes. I stared at them, wondering if they could read minds and I just never knew it. Perhaps they had just known each other that long.

"Your funeral," Malcolm whispered as Chase opened the door. I gulped, wondering what he meant by that.

I stepped inside to find the mansion to be exactly like it had been when we came searching there only a little over a week before. It was beautiful—like something you would see on the outskirts of Paris. I could imagine a king or queen living there—then again, the Duchess was, well, a duchess. She would live somewhere proper like them.

If it weren't for the fact that the Duchess wanted to see me destroyed, and she had taken over Wonderland,

I would have liked to spend more time in this mansion. It was nice and it wasn't every day that one got to explore such a building.

Chase led us up the stairs and into the room where everything went down. As he opened the door, I gasped at what was in the Duchess's hand—it was a scepter with the orb of Wonderland at the end. I was right—she had it nearby her at all times.

Well, at least we knew where it was now.

I had no idea how we were going to get it away from her. She stood there, smiling, her hair in curls and wearing a golden dress like that from 1800s France. There were floral designs embroidered in it, and it was a work of art if it weren't on such a horrible human being. What was even worse was that Kenny, Davis, and Melvin all surrounded her, each of them equipped with a sword at their side. I gulped.

What were we going to do? I could feel any hope I had left start to disintegrate. This was going to be impossible. There was no way we could get past all of them and get the orb.

The Duchess stood tall and smiled. "Dear Alice. It is so nice to see you again."

"I would have to disagree," I stated. "I am not

entirely happy to see you."

She laughed and gestured to her guards—mainly Melvin, Davis, and the others. "Are you not happy to see your friends?"

I shook my head. "No. These aren't my friends. You brainwashed them all to serve you and hate us. Let them go, and I will be happy to see them."

"I don't think I will be doing that anytime soon." She tapped her lips with her gloved hand. "But it is rather boring to have all these people just worship the ground I walk on." She laughed. "Actually, that's a lie. I love it."

Malcolm rolled his eyes. The Duchess sneered at him. "Have something to say, Malcolm?"

"Nothing that you would want to hear, Duchess. I am mainly imagining how I am going to murder you ever so slowly. It almost makes me want to go back to my old ways in the Dark Forest."

Chase nudged him with his elbow, as if telling him to shut up, but Malcolm held the Duchess' gaze. At first she appeared angry but then simply smiled.

"Oh, Malcolm, do you really think such words are going to scare me? You can't win. There is no way you can win at this point. In fact, I am pretty sure you are going to be executed…" She paused and put her finger to her lip. "Tomorrow morning. Yes, that would be perfect. That way I can keep your pretty little head as a trophy."

My eyes widened. She was going to kill him? That couldn't happen—I couldn't lose another person in my life. "No, you can't!"

The Duchess laughed as she patted my face with her gloved hand. "And why not? I am the Duchess, and he is my only enemy." She turned and stood face-to-face with Malcolm. He didn't show any emotion but just stared. "Wouldn't it be ironic? The executioner of Wonderland executed himself?"

Malcolm let a small grin appear on his face. "Do you fear me that much, Duchess? That you would rather have me dead than try to brainwash me like you did the others? Am I too much of a threat?"

She frowned. "You know as well as I that once someone uses the orb, it can't change time and space until it is in Alice's hands. That's why I always have it with me. And I can't do to you what I did to Chase because, well," she leaned in and whispered, "we can't use our magic anymore, can we?"

"I suppose we can't. Not without paying a price."

The Duchess spun and faced me. "Not since dear Alice came and conspired with Howard. And unfortunately even though he died, our powers are still suppressed. It's a shame. I was really hoping his death would help." Her eyes flickered to Chase. "Except for my kitty cat. He can still transport. It is very convenient."

Chase stared at her but didn't say anything. I wondered if Howard was going to suppress Chase's powers like he did the others, but didn't in fear that it would disconnect my world from Wonderland. That, and because it came in handy while moving around.

The Duchess pouted at Chase. "Oh, what is it? Do you hate me now that I have captured your dear little Alice? Did you think she would save you from the mean Duchess who has cursed you?"

Chase turned away, and I felt bad that she would treat someone—the only one who wasn't brainwashed—like that. Then again, he had a spell over him and he couldn't do anything against her. Now I was starting to understand why he didn't say anything. It was impossible to take her down.

No, not impossible. We would do it. It was apparent that Chase wanted to get rid of her. He would help us.

"Now, what to do with my dear Alice." She stepped in front of me. The rose perfume came wafting off her so thick that it made me cough. It was strong and overpowering and started to give me a headache like when I went into the school bathroom and all the girls were applying way more than needed. Two spritzes. That was all anyone required.

She picked a leaf out of my hair. "You are quite filthy, Alice. You must have journeyed far."

"They were with Dodo," Chase answered. "I had a feeling Malcolm would be looking for help outside Wonderland, and I was right."

"So you were." She bit her lip. "So Dodo was going to help you. I should have known. He is such a rascal, even if he's been a hermit for all this time. I suppose if his pupil was Howard, he would be up to the same tricks. I will have to teach him some manners later."

"He didn't help us," I said. "He was just stalling until Chase showed up. You have nothing to scold him for." I didn't know why I was standing up for him, since he really did betray us. Perhaps it was because I could understand why he did it.

"He didn't help you? I guess that makes sense, given everything that Malcolm has done to him. My, my, how the tables have turned, haven't they, Malcolm? Going to people who were once your enemy for help? Only to get stabbed in the back. It must eat you up."

"At least I don't have to brainwash people into being my friend." He smiled.

The Duchess slapped him across the face. "Don't you dare say that after everything you did. You are the reason I was put on trial and almost beheaded!"

I tried to recall the old story. Was that in it? I sort of remembered something about the Duchess being on trial, or maybe it was just Kenny and his tarts. Either way, how dark her eyes were as she glared at Malcolm gave me an idea of how it all went down. The answer was, not well.

"That was a long time ago. Things changed, Duchess. Other than you. You stayed being the horrible human that you are."

She slapped him again. Malcolm didn't waver, even though his cheek was now a bright red.

The Duchess spun on her heels. "Take them to the dungeon! In the morning, Malcolm will be executed, and then I will decide what to do with our dear Alice."

I shouted as Chase grabbed my arm. "No, you can't! I won't help you with anything if you hurt him!"

She laughed. "You don't have much of a say, dear Alice. You are out of luck."

CHAPTER NINETEEN

Chase led us down the stairs and into the basement. The building was the same as it had been when we searched it, except more lively with maids and servants and guards. They all stared as we were brought passed them. I didn't care, though, as I couldn't believe what was happening. Chase had turned us in. Malcolm was ordered to be executed. I couldn't let any of that happen, but what was I going to do? We were severely outnumbered and needed to get the orb back. Was this going to be impossible? Were we really going to have everything end in the morning? I couldn't let Malcolm die. There was no way.

I tried to come up with a plan, but only moments had passed and my mind wouldn't stop racing. We were practically sitting ducks at the moment, just waiting for someone to save us. But would anyone save us? Everyone had been brainwashed so it was only up to us and Chase. After watching him turn us in, I wasn't so sure he would help in the end. It was clear she had him around her finger, whether it was because he also got brainwashed again or if it was due to the curse. Either way, I couldn't count on him. I had to figure this out on my own.

Taking a deep breath, I tried to calm myself. I didn't want to seem like I was having a panic attack around people who used to be my friends. No, I would be strong and get to the cell, and then I would panic. At least Malcolm would be there to calm me down.

I glanced over at Malcolm, who didn't seem worried about all of this. He normally had a poker face on, but I had seen it falter before. Perhaps I didn't have to worry —perhaps he had a plan he hadn't told me. Or perhaps he really just wanted it all to end. I didn't like the last idea and felt that probably wasn't the case. Then again, only a couple of hours ago was when I learned he was actually once human and that was why he didn't want me to stay. It led to many more questions, such as whether or not the others had also been human and why some of them turned into partial animals. But Wonderland never did make sense.

We got to the cell, and Chase pushed me gently forward and closed the door. It was similar to what prison doors one would see in movies set in the 1700s. In fact, It appeared like the cell in *Pirates of the Caribbean*. I glanced around for a dog but didn't see any. I did find that this area was rather clean for a prison. It must have been because the Duchess wouldn't want any part of her mansion dirty, even if it was the prison. On the other side of the prison doors were well painted walls with beautiful landscapes hanging. There was even a vase of flowers on a table.

Chase locked the door. "One of us will always be guarding on the other side of that door. If you try anything, you will be executed on the spot."

I glared at him. "How could you, Chase? You can stop this! Why won't you help us?"

Chase shook his head, his eyes sad but unwavering.

"I can't help you. I'm sorry."

With that, he left us. Once he no longer could see us, I sat down on the hard ground, and tears dropped down from my face.

Malcolm took a seat next to me on the ground. "Don't worry, it will be all right. I'm not that easy to execute; otherwise, many would have already done it."

I shook my head. "No, this is all my fault. You are going to face death because of me. I can't help but be sad and frustrated and mad. None of this should be happening."

"Wonderland repeating history is definitely not your fault. If you weren't here, I guarantee it would still have happened. Just with a different Alice. But the Duchess had this planned for a long time. I doubt any other Alice could have handled it any better."

I let out a little laugh. If all the Alices were similar, then he was probably right. I still didn't understand how I was fated to be here and save Wonderland. It should have been someone cleverer than me. "Why are you always so nice to me? Why don't you get angry? I have caused you nothing but problems!"

He wrapped his arms around me. "Shh. No, you haven't. Now breath, okay? We will get out of this, I promise you. I have a plan."

I wiped away some of the tears. "Oh, and what is that?"

He laughed. "You must be tired and stressed. Didn't you notice what Chase did?"

I glanced around. I didn't see anything out of the ordinary. He had locked the door and I didn't doubt that someone outside was guarding the place. "I have no idea what you are talking about."

Malcolm placed his finger on my hair. "He left you your bobby pins, and this is a classic door that is easy to pick, is it not?"

I gasped. "You are right. Why didn't I think of that?"

"Because a lot has happened. I don't blame you for not noticing. But he definitely knew you had them in there since he was the one who taught you that trick."

I smiled a little as I realized Chase was trying to help us. I began to take out the bobby pins when Malcolm stopped me. "No, wait. Not yet. Right now we are being heavily guarded. No, what we need to do is wait until my execution tomorrow."

"What? Why? Wouldn't it be better to get this over with? Then we can be free?"

Malcolm shook his head. "No, because the Duchess

won't think you will have any way to break free and won't have the others guard you. They will all be at the execution in case I do something. You can sneak out then and get the upper hand. When she isn't looking, grab her staff or whatever and reverse everything. If we try to leave now, it will be much harder."

I knew it was easier said than done, but he had a point. We wouldn't be able to get out of here now, but we would be able to in the morning. I nodded.

"Fine. That sounds like a plan."

"And if you don't show and save the day, I will use my power to stop her."

I stared at him. I couldn't believe what he was saying. "What?"

He stroked my hand with his thumb. "Don't worry, it will be a last resort. But either way, if I have to die, I might as well stop it all."

I shook my head. "I won't let you. I will save you before that happens."

"All right. I will hold you to that." He leaned back on the ground. "But for now, let's get some rest. It has been a very long few days."

I leaned back and lay next to him. He kissed my head. "Good night, Alice. This will be your last night in

Wonderland where you will have to worry. After this, everything will be how it should be. No more dangers. Except the Dark Forest, of course."

I chuckled a little, as that was all I could do other than fear for our lives. He had a point, though. Wonderland had many decades of peace and it would have kept on going if it weren't for the Duchess. If we could finally destroy her, then this world would be free.

I closed my eyes and was surprised at how easy it was for me to fall asleep.

I woke to find Malcolm was already up. He was sitting against the wall next to me, taking long, deep breaths, as if calming himself. His eyes were closed, as he focused on whatever was on his mind. Perhaps he wasn't as confident as I thought he was in this mission. I didn't have confidence in myself either, so I didn't blame him. I wouldn't let him down, however. I would save him. I just had to, or else there would be no way to save Wonderland.

"Hey," I said, which made him open his eyes.

He smiled as he saw I was awake. He stretched his arms up. "Hey. You ready for your big day?"

I shook my head. "Nope, not in the slightest. How

about you?"

"As I said, this isn't my first execution. After one's fifth, they aren't anything special."

I raised an eyebrow. "Fifth?"

"This will be my eighth actually. Two through five were by the Queen of Hearts and six and seven were by the White Queen and then the Red Queen."

"And the first?" I asked, fascinated that one could be executed so many times.

"Medieval Europe. Witch trials."

I was not expecting that. Honestly, I thought it was going to be some horrible tyrant before the Queen of Hearts. "Oh… I'm sorry. That must have been horrible."

"I don't blame them. The illusions you have seen me use in your world, I could use back then. I was a witch, in a sense, and I may or may not have caused a few problems. But just as I was about to be burned to death, I was brought here and given a choice: become the Mad Hatter or go back to be burned to death. I didn't bat an eye when I took it. It was the only way to survive."

So much time had gone by since then, and I could only imagine what he had gone through. "What about the others? I presume they all have similar stories?"

"That they do. There are just some people who aren't right for your world and are meant to live here."

I gave him a look. "Is that so?"

He smiled. "I'm sorry I have made your decision process so much harder. It's just… after so much time, I wanted to make sure you were making the right choice for yourself. Although I would still pick becoming the Mad Hatter, there are times when I wish forever would just end."

I could understand that. Just when I was going to talk more about his past, the doors opened. Melvin stood there in the doorway with Davis and Bill. We didn't have any more time. I should have spent this morning going over what we were going to do, but I had wasted it. That didn't matter, as I knew how to get out of here.

"Your time is up, Malcolm. Say goodbye to your dear Alice."

"Oh, is it morning already?" Malcolm stood up. "I would hate to be late. Speaking of which, where is that little rabbit?"

"He, of course, is going to be your executioner. He is looking forward to putting an end to you after all the trouble you have caused."

A grin appeared on Malcolm's face. "Oh, I bet. I

doubt he is even brainwashed. He's always had it out for me."

Melvin started to take Malcolm away. I tried to walk out of the cell too when Bill shook his head. "Oh no, Alice. You are to stay here like a good girl."

My eyes widened, even though I expected it and needed it to enact my plan. But I could't let them become suspicious. "But he is my love. I can't let him do this on his own!"

"You can, and you will. Don't worry, we will be back in a jiffy to take you to the Duchess. She will have made up her mind what to do with you after Malcolm's execution."

Bill laughed as they escorted Malcolm away.

"No! Please! Don't hurt him!" I screamed after. Bill didn't slow down as he left the room. I kept calling after but couldn't hear anyone after a little while. I stopped yelling and counted to sixty. As I no longer could hear anyone, I pulled out my hairpins and went to work.

CHAPTER TWENTY

I fiddled with the two bobby pins for a bit when I heard the click of the lock. I pushed it open just as a figure appeared in front of me. I jumped back as Chase folded his arms.

"I figured you would be doing something like this." He watched me with his cat-like eyes. His tail wagged back and forth, as if impatient.

I put my hair pins back in my hair. "Well, what am I supposed to do? The boy I love is going to die! I have to save him!"

Chase frowned a little, and I realized why. He still cared about me, but at that moment, I really didn't want to deal with his feelings as he brought all this on himself. He was the reason we were dealing with all of this, even if he was forced to.

He ruffled his hair as he paced back and forth. I eyed the door, debating if I could make it out of here past him. The answer was probably no since he could teleport, but I wouldn't give up without a fight. I couldn't let Malcolm die because of me. I was just about to bolt when Chase started speaking.

"I-I can take you to him."

I stared at him. So Malcolm was right when he saw that Chase didn't take my bobby pins—he was trying to help. But after all this time, it was still suspicious. "What?"

He kept pacing while shaking his head. "I don't... I don't want to live like this anymore. I don't want you to hate me, and I don't want to be under her control. I don't care the cost."

I smiled a little. "While I am glad you decided to help, I still haven't forgiven you. Kate..." I stopped and let out a breath. "Right now we need to focus. Can you take me to where they are?"

"Yes. Then we can st—" Chase knelt down, grimacing as he held his nose and mouth. As he pulled away, blood trickled down his chin from his nose.

I hurried to his side. "What's wrong?"

He wiped away the blood. "Nothing. Don't worry about it. It's just the spell she has over me. I will be fine."

That was why he never tried before. It was killing him. That was why he went to Howard as Howard was one of the few who could use magic.

"Chase…"

"I said I'm fine. Let's go."

I knew this was a lie, but there was no use in arguing. We had to hurry and this conversation could wait. We would figure it out later.

Chase set his hand on my shoulder, and we appeared outside the mansion. The light was bright and it took a moment for my eyes to adjust. The sky was blue with a couple of clouds and the sun shined brightly in the sky. It would be a perfect day if it weren't for the Duchess.

We were behind a crowd that was watching the stage where the Duchess now stood. She was wearing a dress similar to what she wore yesterday, but it was a few shades lighter with tulips embroidered into it. Her hair was done up in curls and if you met her on the street, you would think she was an innocent girl. I knew better, though. We all did. Also on stage were some guards, including Melvin and Davis, and the White Rabbit with a rather large axe. In the center of the stage was Malcolm. He was bound with his arms behind his back. He stared aimlessly in the crowd. I prayed he saw us and wouldn't do something stupid.

I glanced over to Chase who's ears were flickering as the Duchess began talking.

"We are here today to witness the execution of a traitor to Wonderland." She held out her staff at Malcolm. "The Mad Hatter, Malcolm, who was conspiring to kill me."

The crowd half applauded, half were saying, "Boo." I wasn't sure if they were saying boo at Malcolm or at the Duchess, but we crouched down, trying to stay out of sight from the guards and the Duchess. If we wanted to succeed, we would need to get the upper hand.

"So what is the plan?" I asked in a whisper. No one around us seemed to care we were here, but I wanted to be safe.

Chase shrugged. "Not sure. I can— Ah!"

He held his head. Dark red blood dripped down from his nose again..

"Chase, I can't—"

"Well, lookie here."

I glanced up to find Bill with his arms folded, staring down at us. He simply smiled. "Seems we have ourselves an intruder." His eyes flickered to Chase. "And a traitor."

"It just had to be you," Chase commented as he spat out some blood. I didn't know what to do. Something was clearly happening to Chase but no one around us cared. The only person who could do anything was Malcolm and he was currently being executed. I needed to save them both.

Except now Bill was here and he was going to arrest us.

Bill grabbed us both by the collar of our shirts. He called out, "Oh, Duchess! Look what I found!"

The Duchess turned to us and smiled. "Alice. I had hoped you would join the party. Now come watch while the boy you love is executed."

"I will not let you kill Malcolm! Let him go! You have everything you have ever needed. Why do our lives matter so much?" I exclaimed as Bill still held me.

I tugged a little but he wasn't letting up. He learned last time not to get distracted.

I glanced at Malcolm who was holding my gaze. I couldn't decipher his mood from this distance, and whether or not he was mad that I had been caught already. I was frustrated we had been, as I didn't think they were back here. Apparently I was wrong. They knew I would try something. That, or they had their suspicions about Chase and were just waiting.

Either way, I couldn't let this be the end. I would figure out a way to stop everything I loved from being destroyed.

The Duchess laughed. "Because you two are always at the front of putting a wrench in my plans. If I let you go, you will figure out something and destroy everything I have achieved."

Of course I was. She was an evil dictator who only cared about herself. "Then let us go to my world! We won't be able to come back, and you will be safe. Please!"

She laughed again. "Malcolm will not be able to survive in your world once Wonderland is severed on your seventeenth birthday. He wouldn't remain living. 'Tis the curse of being one with roles."

Which was why he said he couldn't stay. It made sense, but I had hoped she would listen to my plea, and we could figure something out there. I noticed people come up to my side. I glanced around to find Kenny on my left with several other guards. I should have figured they would surround me, along with Bill holding us back.

But it wouldn't be enough. All I needed was to get to the stage. I could do it—I could make it past them all and get to Malcolm.

I glanced at Chase and gave him a nod. He frowned a little and then nodded in return. He knew what I needed him to do.

With a swift movement, he kicked Bill in the leg, causing him to loosen his grip enough for me to start running toward the stage. Suddenly Bill disappeared with Chase and they went wherever Chase decided to put them. Moments later Chase appeared again and grabbed Kenny before Kenny could run after me. I didn't look back as I kept running toward Malcolm and the Duchess. Davis and Melvin began to take out their swords when Chase appeared and quickly vanished with them. He came back and grabbed the White Rabbit.

Now no one was there to protect the Duchess. I watched as her eyes widened in surprise, but they quickly turned into a smile.

"Well played, Alice, but I have one more trick up my sleeve."

She pointed the scepter at me, and suddenly lightning came out. So she had lied when she said that she couldn't use it for anything else. I had a feeling she did that so she would catch me by surprise—like she had just now.

I ducked down and rolled into the crowd, praying she wouldn't shoot if her citizens were in front of me. She hesitated at first, but realized I was closing the distance between us. Then she struck whoever was near me without a care. The citizens who were nearby vanished within seconds of getting hit by the lightning. I ran faster, trying not to think about those who were getting killed. I had to keep moving forward or else they all would be destroyed by her selfishness. When I reversed everything she did, I would bring them back. I promised.

I made it to the stage. The Duchess aimed her scepter at me but I quickly shoved her down before she had a chance. She fell back and her layered dress went every which way. Without a second thought, I ran into Malcolm's arms.

"Thank goodness you are safe." I held him tight.

"Yes. Thanks to you."

It was at that moment I realized I made a huge mistake. I couldn't help it, I knew that Malcolm was going to do something stupid if I didn't save him. He was the only thing that was on my mind. It was the laughter of the Duchess that snapped me out of it and realize I didn't take her scepter away from her.

I turned to find her pointing it at the two of us. Her hair was now a mess and her dress was still sort of twisted. She didn't care as her crazed eyes glared at us.

"Silly, silly girl. You are not very smart, now are you? Lucky for me I was up against you instead of the old Alice. Now, say your goodbyes!"

Malcolm wrapped his arms around me and spun so he would take the strike before I did. I knew if it hit him that we were both toast, but feeling his arms around me, I knew I could die happy that we were together for our last breath. Even though it was my fault for being such an idiot and not taking out the Duchess when I had the chance.

Why didn't I listen to Malcolm earlier? Why didn't I trust him to save Wonderland and Kate? Our death was all my fault.

Except the bolt never hit. Instead, there was the sound of gasping coming from the Duchess' direction. Malcolm and I turned to find a sword sticking out of the Duchess's stomach. Blood soaked the blade and started to spread into her light yellow dress. She stared down at it, her eyes wide and confused. Finally, she collapsed to her knees and fell over. Standing behind her, taking deep breaths, was Chase.

Malcolm and I hurried over to where her body lay. Malcolm put his hand on the side of her neck and shook his head. "She's dead."

I put my hand over my mouth and almost started crying. It was over—all of this was over. I glanced over to Chase who was still standing there, breathing hard, staring at the Duchess' lifeless body.

"Chase…" I began when I noticed movement around the stage.

One by one everyone around us shook their heads as if they were waking up from some kind of dream. It was similar to when everyone woke up from the nightmare circus. As they awoke, the world around us began to reshape and form back into what it once was. This was no longer the capital but where the Duchess had her estate. Trees and roads shifted and the sun moved back to where it should have been in the sky. I took a deep breath and smelt the sweet scent of flowers.

Wonderland was back to normal.

"Alice!" Davis yelled as he and the others ran to us. The orb must have brought them back to wherever Chase had taken them. I smiled, happy to see my friends back to normal. Davis wrapped his arms around me. "I'm so glad you are okay."

"I am glad you all are fine. Is everything done? Did we win?"

He nodded. "That we did! She no longer has control over Wonderland! You and Malcolm did it!"

I shook my head. "No, it wasn't us. It was Chase—"

As I said his name and looked up at him, I watched his face turn pale and he collapsed to the ground with a loud thud.

"Chase!" I exclaimed as I rushed to his side. He began to cough and grasp at his throat. Blood sprayed out of his mouth as he kept on gasping for air. My hands shook as I didn't know what to do. He appeared to be in a lot of pain and I had no idea what to do.

Malcolm stepped up to us. "It is the curse the Duchess put on him. He killed her and now he is paying that price."

I looked up at Malcolm, then back down to Chase. "Is this true? Are you…?"

He coughed but was able to answer. "Yes. I disobeyed her. She made it so if I ever did, I would start to die. Seems it was true. I hoped it wasn't but was always too afraid to find out. Howard, though, he knew and tried to sever the link. It was no use apparently."

I shook my head as I knelt down and grabbed his hand. "No, you can't die! You are my friend!"

He smiled as he brushed a piece of my hair away from my face. "It's fine. Wonderland is safe and you are safe. I'm sorry for what I did. If I could go back, I would be braver and tell you all the truth."

He stared at me for a moment longer, a small smile on his lips. After a moment, his eyes turned dim and his hand collapsed to the ground. My eyes filled with tears.

I screamed. "No! I can't lose another friend! No!"

None of the others moved as I cried over Chase. I couldn't believe this was real—I couldn't believe he would die just like that. There had to be a way to save him.

I glanced at the staff that the Duchess still clenched. I quickly plucked the orb off of the end and held it close, summoning whatever power I could.

"Wait, Alice, you heard what Dodo said!" Malcolm warned. "You will never be able to leave Wonderland if you use it."

I nodded my head slowly and sniffled a little. "I know what I am doing, but I can't let them pay this price. I have to save my friends. Besides, I don't think I could go on living in my world knowing the truth."

Malcolm didn't stop me and I could tell Davis and Melvin were not going to get into the middle of us arguing about it. I had made up my mind and they wouldn't be changing it, no matter what any of them said. I was going to save my friends, even if it cost me my life.

I focused all my energy on reviving Chase and bringing back Kate. I closed my eyes and felt the energy of the orb as it became warmer and warmer. Suddenly the sweet scene of flowers was gone and I opened my eyes to find that I was no longer on the mansion ground but in a different area of Wonderland, or at least if it was Wonderland. There were no features of the place but just blue light—almost as if I were in a cloud or a plain room. It was similar to when I was fighting Morpheus and was given the orb, but this felt less being given something and more like it was a test.

As I took a better look around, I found a girl the same age as I wearing a blue dress. This time I wasn't being greeted by a version of myself, but the Alice of legend. My mouth dropped and I stared at her beauty. It was no wonder her and Malcolm were kind of a thing. Her blond hair was long and slightly curled. Her makeup was natural and helped bring out her natural beauty.

She smiled as she looked at me. It was a kind smile, like a grandmother smiling at her grandchildren. "Do you really want to stay here? Everyone in your life on Earth will forget you. They won't know you exist while you will live here forever and ever."

I nodded and kept my ground. This was a test—I had to show that I knew what I was doing and that I was willing to give up my life to save my friends. "It is a choice I am willing to make. Not just for my love of Malcolm but for the lives of my friends."

"But you will never see your family again."

My heart ached a little. I did care about my family, and I would miss them very much, but I couldn't imagine making the choice of them over two friends' lives, not to mention they wouldn't be hurt by my choice. They just wouldn't remember. "I wouldn't be able to see my friends again either way."

Alice smiled. "Then you are able to choose something I could not. You see, this isn't the first time someone not destined for Wonderland made their way here. She was my friend, but I couldn't sacrifice myself for her. I couldn't leave my family."

That was why Malcolm didn't want to bring it up—he knew it was a choice the other Alice had to make as well. "You made the right choice for yourself. But this is the right thing for me to do."

Alice nodded. "Then you will be granted the power. And you will forever be Alice of Wonderland."

There was a bright light and after my eyes adjusted, I was back on the stage. I glanced around to find everyone staring at me. I peered down to find the orb gone. I could feel it this time—it was now inside of me, shining bright. Its connection was even stronger than it had been before. I could tell if we disconnected, I would no longer exist.

It was a strange feeling—especially since at that moment I felt the disconnect from my world. I could remember everything but it was as if that strong tether that once kept me linked to my world was now severed. I knew that no one in my world remembered me. I felt almost relieved, as now I didn't have to worry about them. A tear fell down my cheek as I took a deep breath.

As I looked back up, I found Kate standing there, still in her pajamas, confused. She was searching all around, not knowing why she was in the middle of a stage. More tears started to fall down my face. I had done it— I saved her. I quickly got up and wrapped my arms around her.

"Thank goodness you are safe!"

She was shaking but grabbed on to me. "Alice… what is going on?"

I held her tight and didn't let her go. She was safe and I wouldn't let anything bad happen to her again. "I will explain. Just know you are safe now."

We sat there for a moment when I heard someone start coughing. I turned to find Chase regaining his color. My eyes widened. I was able to save him too. His curse was broken and he was alive. More tears clouded my eyes.

"Chase! You're alive!"

He sat up and rubbed his head. "Apparently. Still feel like crap though. What did you do?"

"I used my power. I brought you and Kate back."

His eyes widened. "But now you will never be able to leave. You shouldn't have done this!"

I turned to Kate. "Give me a second, okay? You are safe now."

She nodded. "Yeah."

I got up and wrapped my arms around Chase. "I had to. I couldn't let you die. Besides, I didn't just do it for you. I was able to bring back two friends."

"Oh…"

I leaned back and whispered in his cat ears, "But I would have done it just for you as well. Just don't tell Malcolm, okay? He wouldn't be that thrilled and would probably take it out on you."

Chase chuckled, then grimaced. "I guess I'm not quite healed yet."

I motioned for Bill. "Bill, can you get him somewhere to treat his wounds?"

"Yes, ma'am."

I smiled and stared at my friends. Everything was finally where it should be.

CHAPTER TWENTY-TWO

Kate and I sat on my bed in the palace. She was wearing a pair of pajamas that Malcolm was able to retrieve. I convinced everyone to let her stay just one night, as everything had been reversed and she had 24 hours before she needed to return. Once she did, our world—her world—would go back to the moment she was taken, and her parents wouldn't have seen she was gone. Bill was the one who was able to calculate that, luckily. I was happy to be able to have one last sleepover with my best friend.

She glanced around, shaking her head. "I can't believe all of this is real. Why did you never tell me?"

I laughed. "Would you have believed me, or would you have said I was reading too much manga and falling asleep with too strong of paint fumes in my room?"

"That's fair." She took in a deep breath. "Honestly I still can't believe it. My best friend is now the Alice of Wonderland."

"The new Alice at least. And the future Alice."

She looked at me quizzically. "What do you mean?"

I opened my mouth, trying to find the right words, when a knock on the door interrupted our conversation.

"May I come in?" Malcolm's voice came from the other side of the door.

I glanced to Kate, who nodded. "Yes!"

Malcolm stepped inside, his arm full of pillows. "I wasn't sure how many you needed so I brought a few."

"Thank you, Malcolm," I said as he set them on the bed.

He kissed the top of my head. "No problem. Now I will let you two have your sleepover."

"Before you go, I had something I needed to talk to

you about Malcolm. Can we talk outside real quick?"

He nodded. "Of course."

I turned to Kate. "It will be just a second. I will be right outside the door."

"Take your time, I will be here."

I smiled and followed Malcolm into the hallways. Shutting the door, I asked Malcolm what was on my mind. "What did you all do with Chase?"

Malcolm let out a sigh. "I should have figured."

"He saved us and risked his life. If it weren't for us getting the orb back, and me already bringing back Kate in exchange for staying here, he would be dead."

"Well, he's a cat so it doesn't matter where we put him as he can get out. So he's in his room and is to report tomorrow morning in the throne room with us as we take Kate back. Then the King and Queen will be discussing his sentence."

"Okay. That's good because I will be there."

"But he did commit treason and might get off very lucky."

"And he helped save Wonderland, don't forget that part."

"But he also almost destroyed Wonderland, so don't forget that part."

I gave him a look then changed the subject. "I don't know how to tell Kate that I won't be returning with her."

Malcolm placed his hand on my shoulder. "Live in the moment, Alice. My recommendation would be to tell her tomorrow and just enjoy tonight."

I nodded. "Right. Just enjoy tonight."

"If you need anything, I will be in my room. Just have fun, okay?"

"I will."

With that, I went back into my room. Kate was still hanging out on the bed, but now was collapsed on her back.

"Alice, this bed is amazing! It is the comfiest thing I have ever laid on."

I jumped on the bed next to her. "Right? I love it."

She rolled over so she could face me. "So, this explains a lot. With Malcolm, I mean."

I smiled a little. "Yeah, it was kind of complicated. Still is, in a way."

"Because he's a person from another world and not from ours?"

Right. She didn't know I had to stay. I nodded. "Yeah. We will make it work though. Or at least I hope so."

She didn't say anything but grabbed a pillow that Malcolm had brought and smacked me with it. The soft fabric hit me straight in the face. I gasped and laughed as I grabbed mine and smacked her with it.

It was moments like these that I was going to miss.

After a bit of goofing around, Kate and I laid on the bed, still giggling up a storm. After a moment, Kate spoke up.

"I can see why you spent so much time here and with those guys. You seem a lot more relaxed and free here. This place is where you truly belong."

I turned to face her. "You think so?"

"Yeah. You weren't meant for what others consider to be a normal life. This extraordinary place is where you truly belong."

I frowned a little. It felt nice that she was telling me this, but the truth was she didn't realize that if I stayed here, I could never go back. Not after what I did. It didn't matter, as I didn't have a choice anymore. I saved both her and Chase and I would pay the price.

Her lips curled a little. "Now, tell me, was there anything ever going on with you and Chase?"

I hesitated. Her eyes got big. "I knew it."

I shook my head. "No, it's not what you think. I care about him, but not like I care about Malcolm. And… I'm sorry… for what he did. It was my fault. The Duchess forced him to use you as bait. He tried to tell me but I didn't… He couldn't disobey her without being tortured or even killed. He actually sacrificed himself to save Wonderland."

"I know. Don't worry, I'm not mad at him. Not anymore. After hearing what happened from both you and Malcolm, I get why he did what he did. And I trust you to know him better than I do. But I can see why Malcolm doesn't care for him."

"Yeah. There is still a lot I don't know about them, what happened in their past, and this world, but I will learn and grow with it."

"So you are staying."

Whoops. I let it slip. "Yeah… I am."

She grabbed my hand and squeezed it tight. "Will I ever see you again."

I knew I should tell her the truth right then and there, but I couldn't bring myself to do it. "Of course."

She smiled. "Well, then maybe we should get to sleep. You have had a long few days, or weeks, or however much time has passed."

Kate was right, but I didn't want to sleep as these would be the last few hours I would get to be with her. However, my body disagreed and the moment I closed my eyes, I fell right to sleep.

We gathered in the old capital palace where the king and queen of dreams awaited. Kate was back in her old pajamas so her family wouldn't wonder why she had a set of clothes they had never seen before. Kate and I bowed to the king and queen. Her eyes were wide, as she had never met royalty before. I held her hand, letting her know I was there.

"Alice," the Queen began as the White Rabbit stayed close. He didn't seem to want to leave her side ever again. I couldn't blame him. "You have once again saved Wonderland and at the cost of living your life here. It won't be easy, as many will be after you for what you possess."

I nodded. "I am well aware of that, Your Majesty, but I had to save my friends. I can't imagine a life without them."

"Well, you saved all of this. But now you must leave your friend as it is the price you paid."

I peered over at Kate, who appeared a little confused

by what the queen meant. I couldn't imagine this goodbye, and yet it was before us.

I nodded. "Of course. But before we go on, can I make one request?"

"Oh? What is that?"

"Please wipe any charges that Chase will be facing. It is all I ask for having saved this wonderful kingdom."

The Queen eyed me. "He committed treason."

"Who hasn't in Wonderland?"

She held her gaze for a moment longer, then smiled. "It is done. Now say your goodbyes as we ready the Looking Glass."

I turned to Kate and tears started to appear in her eyes. She whispered, "you lied when you said I would see you again, didn't you?"

I nodded. "I'm sorry. I just couldn't bring myself to tell you the truth."

Her eyes teared up. "But this place is so dangerous. How can you tell me you will be fine?"

I glanced over at Malcolm and the others. "Because I have friends who will always have my back."

She peered over at them and smiled a little. "I guess you are right. This makes perfect sense, you know? I said this before, but still… I always wondered what it was you were keeping from me. I couldn't ever imagine…" She laughed. "You are right. You do belong here. But I don't think I can live knowing I won't see you again. And what about your family?"

I hesitated. "Kate, there is something else I didn't tell you. When you go through the Looking Glass and the link between worlds is finally disconnected… no one will remember me in our world."

Her eyes widened. "What? No. That is even worse! Well, not for everyone else, but it is for me! I don't want to forget all our memories!"

I hugged her. "It will be all right. You will go on to be some great track runner and incredible genius of some sort, and I will be here, keeping Wonderland safe. We will both have great lives."

She pulled me in tightly. We held each other's embrace for a while before someone interrupted.

"Alice, it is time." The White Rabbit interrupted us. He was never good at picking up social cues. I would have to work on that with him.

We moved to the Looking Glass, and Kate and I gave each other one last hug. "I love you, Kate."

"I love you too, Alice. Be safe, all right?"

I nodded, tears falling down my face. "You too."

And with that, she stepped through the Looking Glass. I watched as the reflection turned back to normal, and something inside me felt the severing of the connection between worlds.

It was like heartstrings snapping.

Malcolm stepped up next to me. "She will be all right."

I nodded. "Yeah, she will."

"And you have us for anything you need."

I turned to find everyone smiling. Davis added, "That's right, Alice. We will always be here for you."

Chase nodded with a sad smile on his face. I could tell he still felt responsible, but he stuck around for me. "All of us."

I grinned, happy that my friends were finally safe and we could begin a new adventure all over again.

CHAPTER TWENTY-THREE

Kate shut her locker and headed to AP European History class. She passed her track friends and waved good morning. She felt a bit out of it, as if the dream she had last night had left her tossing and turning. But it almost felt as if the dream she had were real, but what was it?

She passed familiar faces, all of whom she had known for the past three years, if not longer. It was a daily occurrence—seeing these faces and going through the motions of school. Except it was as if she was missing something. Everyone around her was moving as smoothly as it normally did, and yet something was wrong. She stopped for a moment and peered around. A senior brushed shoulders with her as everyone was hurrying to get to class. I too needed to hurry.

Perhaps it was just because it was a new year, Kate thought to herself. Now she had AP classes and college was just on the horizon. She was no longer an underclassman but had students look up to her that she helped tutor. Perhaps that was why everything felt different and that was what was suddenly hitting her.

Kate entered AP European History class. The class would be traveling to Europe next month and she could hardly wait. Today they would go over some of the itinerary. She sat down at her desk in the front and grabbed a pencil out of her pouch.

"Hey, do you need a pencil?" she asked as she turned to the seat next to her. There was no one there. In fact, no one had ever sat there all term.

Kate smiled to herself as her heart warmed with a

tinge of pain.

<u>THANK YOU FOR READING</u>

Thank you so much for reading! Readers like you make it possible for authors like me to write stories! If you could spare a moment and leave a review on Amazon, Goodreads, BookBub, and wherever you like to buy books, that would mean the world to me! It really helps authors like me to succeed in the publishing world.

Continue reading to get a sneak peak of THE QUEST, a YA sci-fi adventure!

THE QUEST

SANSHLIAN SERIES: BOOK 1

DANI HOOTS

Eleven Years Earlier

It sounded like thunder, but I knew better. War had made its way to our tiny planet and nothing could stop it. I sniffed and wiped away the tears beginning to form in my eyes as I peered over at my brother Rik. All I could see was his shaggy hair as he peeked out the window, watching the flashes of light that echoed through the sky. I feared for my family's safety, not knowing what we would do. Even at the age of six, I understood what was coming.

"It's all right Arcadia, you don't have to be afraid." My father sat down on the edge of my bed. He always kept calm in every situation, no matter the difficulty. A smile never seemed to leave his face.

"Father," I began as I glanced out at the flashing lights, "will you tell us another story?"

Father scooted closer and wrapped his arm around me, stroking my long brown hair. "I presume you want to hear another story about the legend of Sanshli?" Rik and I nodded our heads in unison, making our father laugh. He pulled out his pocket watch to check how late it had gotten. "Okay, I guess I can tell you one more story before you two need to go to sleep."

Rik climbed in bed next to me and our identical green eyes shone innocently as we waited for our father to start the story.

"A long time ago, there was a planet full of people that looked just like you and me," he began, stretching out his arm for dramatic effect.

"But they weren't like us, were they father?" my brother stated the obvious. I rolled my eyes at him. He always had to interrupt the story with obvious remarks.

Father just smiled. "No Rik, they weren't. They were special. Each person had a unique power. Some could read minds, others could control different elements. But of them all, the most powerful were the illusionists. These illusionists could control anything they wanted, from the elements to the stars themselves. They could perform spells, and if enough of them came together, they could be unstoppable.

"Then one day, the rest of the people decided they'd had enough of the illusionists and their spells. A war broke out. Even though the illusionists were more powerful than the rest of the Sanshlians, there weren't as many of them and they were defeated. The others burned their spell books and left them powerless. The only things they could do were small illusions, like little magic tricks. All the people looked at them with disgrace, and the citizens banished them from the cities. The illusionists traveled around their planet putting on shows for those who wanted to see the simple tricks they could still perform.

"Then, hundreds of years later, one illusionist by the name of Nygard found an old book in a cave. He brought it back to his small camp and found out it was one of the old spell books that were supposedly destroyed centuries earlier. He and his wife Violet got into a big argument as to what to do with the book. She wanted to destroy it and he wanted to use it to become powerful like their ancestors once were. He felt betrayed by her. Do you know what happened next?"

"Nygard became powerful like the old illusionists!" I blurted out. Father chuckled and rubbed the top of my head.

"Yes Arcadia, he became powerful. Very powerful. In fact, he became immortal. People feared him, even his wife Violet. She ran away and hid their daughter because she knew once her daughter became old enough, she would be the only one powerful enough to stop him. This angered him even more and that made his power grow, causing him to become unstoppable.

"The people tried to defeat him, but it was no use. He killed his fellow illusionists with his wrath, and the entire planet turned into chaos. Some even tried to flee the planet, but they didn't get far before Nygard found them and killed them too. He took over the First Republic and made it into the New Empire, declaring himself the Emperor.

"It took many years for Violet to find the right spell to stop him. She tricked him into coming back to Sanshli, and she cast her spell at last. Using a magical sword, she stabbed him through the heart, trapping him in a statuesque form forever. All the chaos had finally ended."

Rik jumped up on the bed as Father finished. "But that's not the end of the story, is it?"

Father leaned in closer to us and whispered. "No. Now legend has it, that whoever finds Sanshli and takes the sword out of Nygard's statue can change the past and make what was once wrong right again."

Rik jumped up and down on my bed, talking about how one day he would find Sanshli and save the universe. I lay there, a thought running through my mind.

"What happened to the baby girl?" I asked.

Father looked at me with bewilderment. Neither of us had ever asked about her, at least that I could remember. I don't know why I never thought to ask before that moment. "No one knows. It remains a mystery to this day," he stroked my cheek. "I think she is still in hiding so that one day she will finish the story."

Our father stood up, stretching his aging limbs. He worked as a farmer, harvesting fruits from our orchard and selling them at a shop in town. Rik, who was three years older than I, helped Father work in the orchard. I still wasn't old enough, being only six. Instead I stayed in the house, keeping it clean and making some meals as I waited anxiously for them to return home each day. Father's friend John would come by on some days and watch me, but most days I was alone. I didn't mind; I always found something to do.

Father pulled out two keys, each hanging from a separate string, out of his coat pocket and enclosed them in our hands. "I want you two to have these and keep them safe."

I examined the key closely. Nothing seemed special about it; it was just an old key. "What are these for Father?"

"They are for the future, Arcadia. Promise me you will keep them safe," he kissed me on the forehead and then did the same to Rik's. "Now, go to sleep you two."

We nodded as Father blew out the candles next to our bed and shut us in our room for the night. Rik climbed into his own bed and glanced out the window. We both knew we wouldn't be sleeping much that night, not with the war slowly engulfing the planet.

Our planet, Garvner, stood no chance against the Pandronan Empire in this war. The planet was once independent of the Empire, held together by treaties and trading contracts. But they wanted more. They wanted control over everything we did and they would have that control soon. Our father assured us that everything would turn out for the best, but we knew deep-down things would change, that we all had a hard road ahead of us. So that is why he told us stories of Sanshli, to get our minds off the war that was happening all around us and to have hope that someone could change everything.

Father loved his stories about Sanshli. Rik and I both knew he dreamt one day he would find the planet Sanshli and be able to change history so that the Pandronan Empire never came into existence. He wished for the Second Republic to still reign as it did so many years ago. But being a poor farmer and father, he knew that he couldn't run off to find some legend. He had to provide for both Rik and me, especially after our mother died. So he filled our heads with the legends and hoped that one day we would find it for him.

Hours passed as we lay in our beds trying to sleep with sounds of gunfire thundering through the city. It sounded like it kept getting louder and louder. Darkness still filled the skies when Father raced into our rooms.

"Arcadia, Rik, wake up!" He pulled us up out of our beds. I rubbed my eyes and looked up at my grin-less father. I had never seen him so serious and at that moment I knew our lives would never be the same. The sound grew with time, each explosion shaking our windows. He grabbed the keys he had given us and stuffed them into our hands.

"Don't lose these, please," he whispered, more to himself than to us.

"Father, what is it?" I asked as we headed down the wooden stairs.

"The war has made it through the city and into the forest. I hoped it wouldn't come this far, but I am afraid they have found us. We must go."

He rushed us towards the backdoor that led into our cherry orchard. The crisp spring night air filled my lungs and I watched as the pink blossoms danced in the wind like snow on a winter's day. I always loved to admire their beauty, but now I didn't have the time. Now fear captured my heart as I looked out at the black abyss that lay ahead of me.

"John is waiting for us on the other side of the orchard." He knelt down next to me and handed me his pocket watch. "Arcadia, I want you to have this. Keep it with you at all times. Never forget everything I have told you. Rik will lead you to Uncle John and I will be right behind you. Now go," he said as he hurried us outside.

The three of us ran through the orchard, Rik in front of me and Father a few meters behind, keeping an eye on the Imperials that were now bombarding our home. We could hear shouts of men ordering the house and everything around it to be searched. Voices presented themselves all around us. I inhaled deeply, trying to catch my breath as I ran harder and harder. The only thing that kept me going was knowing how badly Father insisted that I run for my life. I glanced behind my back to make sure he still followed. He did.

The sound of gunfire echoed through the orchard, bouncing off tree after tree. Shadows loomed over us and my imagination got the better of me. The images looked like the monsters of all the bedtime stories Father had told us. I felt tears form in my eyes as I followed my brother along what seemed like a never-ending trail. I didn't remember the orchard being so big until that day. I watched as the bullets appeared like ghosts, raining upon objects around me; branches, roots, grass, but never me. They scattered in all directions. That's when my worst fear happened. I heard my father let out an agonizing shout of pain. I turned back to find him collapsed on the ground.

"Father!" I called out as I hurried to his side and watched a flood of red liquid soak his shirt around the wound.

"Arcadia, leave me, go! Get out of here!" he tried to wave me to go.

"No, I can't leave you Father, I don't want to leave you." I felt tears run down my face.

"We will see each other in another life, dear daughter. Please, follow Rik and go. Remember everything that I have taught you." he coughed and clenched my hand for the last time. "Don't forget I love you."

I nodded. "I love you too, Father. I will never forget."

Standing up, I started after my brother, but it was too late. I felt someone grab me. In the moment's surprise, I dropped the key. I tried to grab for it, but it was too late. I still clutched the pocket watch in my hand. I screamed and kicked, but it was no use. I could see Rik coming back for me, but I shook my head.

"Rik, run!" I shrieked.

Stopping for a moment and examining the trouble I had gotten into, he turned around and kept running.

A guard checked over my Father's body. "Yes, this is Ben Archer, the resistance leader that the men revealed to us. You two—go after that boy, he is probably his son. We have his daughter."

Two men chased after Rik into the darkness as I struggled with the soldier that carried me off towards the city.

Acknowledgements

I want to thank everyone who made this novel possible. A thank you to Annie at Victory Editing for helping with this project and to Tamara for helping me with content edits. Thank you to Biserka Designs for the amazing covers they have done for my books. And lastly, thank you to my husband and parents who are always supporting me.

I also want to say thank you to Becca at Tippy Toe Dance studio for letting me use you and your studio in my book! And a thank you to Scott and Maria at Escape Fiction for letting me include you in my book as well! My high school years were amazing because of all three of you, and I am glad I got to include it in this series!

About the Author

Dani Hoots is a science fiction, fantasy, romance, and young adult author who loves anything with a story. She has a B.S. in Anthropology, a Masters of Urban and Environmental Planning, a Certificate in Novel Writing from Arizona State University, and a BS in Herbal Science from Bastyr University.

Currently she is working on a YA urban fantasy series called Daughter of Hades, a YA urban fantasy series called The Wonderland Chronicles, a historic fantasy vampire series called A World of Vampires, and a YA sci-fi series called Sanshlian Series. She has also started up an indie publishing company called FoxTales Press. She also works with Anthill Studios in creating comics through Antik Comics.

Her hobbies include reading, watching anime, cooking, studying different languages, wire walking, hula hoop, and working with plants. She is also an herbalist and sells her concoctions on FoxCraft Apothecary. She lives in Phoenix with her husband and visits Seattle often.

Feel free to email her with any questions you might have! danihootsauthor@gmail.com

www.ingramcontent.com/pod-product-compliance
Lightning Source LLC
Chambersburg PA
CBHW070320190726
48291CB00014B/2418